Sew Zoey

on Pins
and
needles

written by
Chloe Taylor

illustrated by
Nancy Zhang

Simon Spotlight

New York London Toronto Sydney New Delhi

SIMON SPOTLIGHT
An imprint of Simon & Schuster Children's Publishing Division
1230 Avenue of the Americas, New York, New York 10020
Copyright © 2013 by Simon & Schuster, Inc.
All rights reserved, including the right of reproduction in whole or in part in any form.
SIMON SPOTLIGHT and colophon are registered trademarks of Simon & Schuster, Inc.
Text by Lara Bergen
Designed by Laura Roode
For information about special discounts for bulk purchases, please contact Simon & Schuster Special Sales at 1-866-506-1949 or business@simonandschuster.com.
Manufactured in the United States of America 0413 OFF
First Edition 10 9 8 7 6 5 4 3 2 1
ISBN 978-1-4424-7936-4 (pbk)
ISBN 978-1-4424- 7937-1 (hc)
ISBN 978-1-4424- 7938-8 (eBook)
Library of Congress Catalog Card Number 2013935205

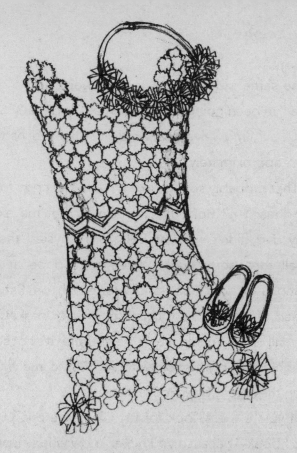

--------- CHAPTER 1 ---------

Plenty of Pom-Poms!

Three guesses where I'm going today—and the first two don't count. The Eastern State University football game, you say? Congratulations! You are right! And, no, I am not wearing this "pom-pom dress." It's what I *wish* the ESU cheerleaders could be wearing instead of the same old uniforms they've been sporting ever since I've been going to their games. And that's . . . let's see . . . If I'm twelve years old . . . that means twelve years, approximately.

That probably sounds like I'm a huge, crazy football fan, doesn't it? But I'm not really, so let me explain. If my dad didn't work at ESU as a physical therapist for all the sports teams, trust me, I'd be at home sewing and sketching (and blogging!) on Saturdays instead of watching a football game—or basketball or baseball . . . You name it and we're there. It's not so bad, though, when my friends Kate and Priti come with me, which they are today. Hooray!

If you're there, look for us. I'll be the one with the sketchbook—because you never know when inspiration will hit! Oh, and I'll be wearing the top that I finally finished, which I blogged about yesterday. Some might think it's a little fancy for a football game, but I think it's just too cute not to wear right away. Too bad I didn't make it Eagles colors—purple and yellow. Hmm. Those colors look pretty good together. Something to think about . . . !

TTFN. Go, Eagles!

(Did I really just say that?! OMG! I better go sew something, so I feel like myself again.)

"Here it comes! Here it comes!" said Priti Holbrooke. She pointed to the end of the football field.

"I see it." Zoey Webber leaned forward and perched on the edge of the metal seat.

On her other side was Kate Mackey, whose big blue eyes were focused on the game. Zoey nudged her. "It's coming. Get ready," she said.

"What?" Kate turned to look. "*Again?*" She groaned, but she was smiling as she leaned forward as well.

A second later, the wave reached them. They stood and threw their arms into the air: Kate's long, tan ones; Zoey's pale, freckled ones; and Priti's, which were cinnamon brown.

"Whooo!" Zoey yelled—not quite as loud as Priti, but close—then they all sat back down and watched the wave continue around.

"That's fifteen!" Priti exclaimed. "How high do you think it'll go?"

Kate glanced at the clock. "Well, it's almost half-time, so it'll have to stop pretty soon."

Suddenly, the crowd jumped back up and an even louder cry rang out. Zoey looked down to see the whole ESU team celebrating what must have been an exciting touchdown.

"Oh! I missed it!" cried Kate. She shook her head in disbelief.

Zoey rubbed Kate's shoulder. "Sorry," she said. Kate took sports very seriously, and since Zoey took fashion very seriously, she knew how she must feel. Not as bad, of course, as Zoey had felt when the dress she'd designed and sewn for their school's fashion show was *mysteriously* ruined by yellow paint. More like when she realized she'd mixed up the sleeves on the top she was wearing that day. She'd almost cried when she had to rip them out and start all over again. In the end, though, it turned out fine. Better than she'd hoped. The top was supersimple . . . *looking*. Basically, a loose-fitting tee. The fabric, though, was a fabulous blue-and-green pattern for the bodice and a magenta-and-gold one for the sleeves.

"Don't worry, they'll do it again," she told Kate.

"Let's hope so," Kate said as she looked at the scoreboard, which now read: VISITORS 21, ESU EAGLES 6.

Priti leaned over Zoey to give Kate a pat on the knee. "Spirit!" she said. "That's what wins games. Hey! You want some stickers to put on your cheeks?" She pointed to her own cheeks, on which tiny gold eagles were perched, and flashed her signature wide Holbrooke grin. "Oh, look out, look out!" she said suddenly. "Here comes another wave!"

By halftime the wave count was twenty. The score hadn't changed. And Zoey was getting hungry. It seemed like way more than two hours since she'd had lunch at home with her dad.

"Snack bar?" she asked her friends, who each instantly jumped up.

"You read my mind! I'm starving," said Kate, already scooting toward the aisle.

Zoey stopped in front of her dad, who'd been sitting behind them with friends from work. They were all wearing ESU caps, which were purple with gold letters across the front. Only her dad had on

The Tie, though, which he always wore for good luck. It was bright purple with gold winking eagles, and frankly it made Zoey's eyes hurt.

Zoey loved her dad more than anything . . . but he was style challenged, to say the least. She sometimes wondered if her mom were alive, would he have still worn the things he did? Zoey was too young when her mom died to remember her well, but everyone still talked about her style and how chic she always looked.

In fact, Zoey wondered a lot of things about what having her mom would be like.

"Hey, Dad? Okay if we go get some popcorn?" she called to him.

He nodded. "Sure. Bring some back for me?"

Zoey held out her hand and opened and closed it, the international sign for *Money, please.*

"Thank you!" she said as he handed her a bill.

"Yeah, thanks, Mr. Webber!" Priti and Kate chimed in.

Together, they hurried down the bleacher steps to the nearest snack bar. The air smelled of salty popcorn and greasy hot dogs, and the line was already long. Zoey read the menu to see what else they might want. . . .

"Ooh, look!" she said. "They have gummy bears!"

Kate made a face, and so did Priti, and Zoey quickly remembered why. Both of her friends had braces, which made gummy bears—and a million other things—almost impossible to eat. Kate had been the first one to get them, and Zoey still remembered how jealous she'd been. "Why can't I get braces?" she'd asked her dad again and again.

"Because you don't need them," he'd told her proudly. "You have straight teeth—like your mom." Personally, Zoey would rather have gotten her mom's strawberry-blonde hair instead of the wavy brown stuff she got from her dad. But she also knew now that braces weren't half as much fun as she'd thought they were when she was ten.

"Popcorn's bad enough," said Priti. "I still have some stuck in my mouth from last week."

"I know." Kate nodded. "I'm going to be so happy on Monday. I can't wait!"

"Monday?" Priti flashed a sneaky look at Zoey. *"Why?"* she asked. "What happens then?"

Kate's mouth fell open, stunned. "I'm getting my braces off. How could you forget?"

"Oh right." Priti nodded this time. "Of course. Silly me." She started to smile at Zoey, but Zoey had to look away. She knew if her eyes met Priti's right then, she could easily blow their surprise for Kate.

"You know, it's too bad Libby couldn't come," Zoey said, since changing the subject seemed like a good idea. Plus, she really was sorry their newest friend from school wasn't there with them too.

Libby was new to Mapleton Prep. She'd just moved to town. And she was one of several happy surprises middle school had brought to Zoey that year. Another was something Zoey had actually petitioned for the year before: For the first time in sixty-five years, no more school uniforms! Now, instead of pleated skirts and ties, students could wear (practically) anything at all, and Zoey was already making the most of the new and much-improved dress code.

Zoey wanted her clothes to say something distinctive about herself. She also believed that clothes were *fun*—not just to wear, but to design. Over the summer, she started sketching all kinds of cool dresses and outfits, though it was a hobby she'd kept to herself. And then one day she showed Kate and Priti—her bestest and oldest friends—and, well, they went kind of crazy over all of them. It was their idea, in fact, for Zoey to put her sketches into her very own fashion blog. And now Sew Zoey had hundreds of followers . . . which was definitely the most surprising surprise of the fall. And every time she looked at the ticker counting visitors to the blog, it was moving ahead.

The line for the concession stand, meanwhile, was barely moving at all.

"Where's Libby, anyway?" Priti asked.

"Remember? Her aunt is visiting this weekend," Zoey said. "But I told her there'd be *lots* more chances to come to a game with us, if my dad has anything to do with it." She laughed.

"And Marcus? I thought he was a big fan?" asked Kate.

"Band practice," Zoey replied. Her brother was sixteen years old and played drums in a band with his friends. They were pretty good but only knew a few songs from start to finish.

"I don't know about you, but I'm happy it's just us. It's kind of nice," said Kate.

"Group hug!" yelled Priti as she pulled Kate and Zoey in for a squeeze. The three girls were still laughing as the line moved up.

At last they got to the counter, and Zoey ordered two popcorns and a drink. "Oh, and a cotton candy," she added.

"Make that two cotton candies!" said Kate. "You know, I think maybe I should go to the bathroom. . . . Anyone else have to go?"

Priti shook her head, and Zoey did as well.

"Go ahead," Priti said. "We'll wait here for you."

Zoey slipped her change in her pocket and watched Kate walk off. "She's going to *love* our surprise!" she said, turning to Priti. "I can't wait until Monday! Oh wait, Tuesday, I guess." That was the day they'd give Kate a gift to celebrate her newly straightened teeth: a "bye-bye braces" lunch bag filled with the things she'd been missing so much for the past two years.

"I already got a ton of stuff!" said Priti. "Have you made the bag?"

"Not yet," Zoey said. "I still have to get the fabric. I was going to get it tomorrow when we go to A Stitch in Time. You're still coming with me to Cecily Chen's book signing, right?"

"Definitely!" said Priti. "I can't wait. I love her clothes!"

"I know," said Zoey. "I can't believe she's from around here!"

Cecily Chen was a young designer, but she was becoming famous very fast. She'd been a judge on *Fashion Showdown* and dressed Kate Middleton several times. Her style was distinctive but always evolving. That season, she was into warm colors and layered pieces that looked effortless, but that were actually pretty complicated to make. But what made Zoey most excited by her was the fact that she'd grown up just two towns away.

According to Jan, who owned the fabric store called A Stitch in Time, the designer had shopped in her store all the time until she got her big break and moved to New York. It gave Zoey a little thrill from then on, whenever she walked through the heavy glass doors. *I'm walking in a famous designer's footsteps!*

"So Kate's not coming?" asked Priti.

"No, she has a soccer game, luckily. Hey! If you want, I can show you my sketch for the bag. . . ."

"Oh good!" Priti took the tray of refreshments from Zoey's hands. "Do it, but make it fast!"

Quickly, Zoey pulled out her sketchbook from her own bag and flipped it open to show Priti the page. "See, it kind of looks like a big lunch bag—but with a curved flap, so it looks like a smile when it's closed."

"Ooh! That's going to be good! Promise you'll make me one too, when my braces come off," she begged.

"Of course!" Zoey told her.

"I'm back," Kate said suddenly.

Zoey and Priti both looked up from Zoey's open sketchbook to see Kate standing there, smiling at them.

"The line was way too long. What're you looking at?" she asked.

"Huh? Oh . . . nothing . . . ," Zoey faltered. She turned the page as fast as she could. "Just got an urge to sketch something . . ." She grinned at Kate. "You know me!"

"Here?" Kate's head swiveled, taking in the jeans-and-sweatshirt-wearing crowd. "What are you going to make now?" she asked. "A football jersey dress?"

Zoey laughed. Then she stopped and put a finger to her chin. "Actually . . . ," she said, "that's a pretty cool idea!"

------- CHAPTER 2 -------

The Joys of Jersey

Remember when I said you never know when inspiration is going to hit you? Well, after the football game on Saturday, I just couldn't get this jersey dress idea out of my mind. I'm thinking of it as a riff on a team jersey that's also *made* of jersey material. It's jersey times two! Anyway, I started wondering why so many things are called "jersey," and that made me think about other kinds of sports jerseys. So, for your viewing pleasure, today's sketch is about as sporty as Sew Zoey gets!

After all that jersey talk, it turned out I don't actually have any in the ESU team colors. So I found some purple gabardine and yellow ribbon for the stripes. It's not going to be exactly like I planned, but I think it's coming together. That's what I love about making clothes: all the happy surprises that it brings! Of course, it can also bring unhappy surprises, as you've read in this very blog. But that's when I try to remember what my dad always says about "looking on the bright side."(Don't tell him I said so, but he's totally right.)

But enough about that . . . I'm about to meet one of my fashion idols in person! This has got to be, hands down, one of the most exciting days of my whole life— right up there with the breakfast with Cinderella in her castle in Disney World (What can I say? I was five.) and the very first day my aunt Lulu took me to A Stitch in Time. Today I'm going to A Stitch in Time—but not to buy fabric, necessarily. I'm going to see Cecily Chen— yes, that Cecily Chen!—who'll be signing copies of her brand-new book. Now the only question is: *What to wear?* Whatever it is, I hope Cecily Chen likes it! What an amazing night this is going to be!

Five o'clock . . . *Ugh,* thought Zoey. Her aunt Lulu should have been there to pick her up by then.

Still waiting, she texted Priti.

Ready when u r, Priti texted back.

Cecily Chen's book signing started at six, and they still had to pick up Priti.

Zoey bet that the line to get books signed was already snaking out A Stitch in Time's front door. She was trying to keep herself busy by putting the finishing touches on a new dress, one inspired by Kate at the football game the day before.

"You're still here?" Her dad walked out of the kitchen and into the dining room, which was more like Zoey's sewing room these days. The table made a great surface for cutting out patterns and fabric (much better than her bed). Plus, the truth was they hardly ever ate in there. Aunt Lulu did all the big family dinners at her house. The room had hardly been used since Zoey was a baby and her mom had sewed in there herself.

Zoey's dad was happy to let her use the room as her mom had. "Besides, if you sewed in your room," he told her, "it would distract you from your home-work even more than blogging does."

"Yeah, I do kind of get in the zone when I sew, don't I?" Zoey said shyly.

"Time flies when you're having fun," he replied. "Hey, I thought you were leaving a half hour ago."

Zoey shrugged. "So did I." She picked up her phone and checked the screen. "I texted Aunt Lulu, and she hasn't texted back, so hopefully she's in the car and almost here." She nodded to the foamy drink her dad was holding. "Who's *that* for?" she asked. It looked like a milkshake . . . in a way. The grayish-green, zombie-skin color, though, made Zoey think again.

"This," her dad said, "is for Marcus. He's study-ing for a test tomorrow, and I thought I'd make him a little energy juice."

"Oh yeah?" *Oh boy*. Her dad and his juicer. "What's . . . in it?" Zoey asked.

He frowned. "Don't look so scared. It's all good stuff," he said.

"Like?"

He grinned. "A banana."

"And?"

"Some apple . . . a carrot . . . some spinach . . ."

Ew.

"Soy milk . . . green-tea powder . . . Oh, and a little ginger to spice it up. Seriously, it's delicious! Here, taste it, Zo," he said.

"That's okay—"

Ding-dong.

Zoey jumped up. Saved by the doorbell!

"That's Aunt Lulu! I'll see you later—after dinner. Tell Marcus bon appétit for me, Dad!"

"I'm so sorry I'm late," said Aunt Lulu as soon as Zoey opened the door. "A client called and like a dope I answered, and she went on and on and *on*. And then Draper had to go out *again*, and that took forever, of course."

Draper was Aunt Lulu's dog and faithful companion since before Zoey was born. She remembered racing with him when she was little for hours around the yard. Now, though, he had two speeds: superslow and comatose.

"But don't worry," Aunt Lulu went on. "We'll be there in plenty of time. Well, *well*!" She paused and crossed her arms. "Don't *you* look adorable, Zo!"

Zoey smiled. "Thanks," she said. "It took me forever to decide what to wear. I almost went with shorts and tights and Cecily Chen-ish layers on top . . . but I then I thought, no, why not wear something I made . . . and I really love this top."

"It's great," said Aunt Lulu. Then she pointed to Zoey's top. "Is that the ikat fabric I gave you?"

Zoey nodded back. "Uh-huh."

"Well, I knew it looked good in my client's living room," her aunt said, "but it looks even better on you—and with that skirt. So cute! So? Are you ready?" She stepped back out through the doorway.

"Oh yeah!" Zoey said. "Oh wait!" She turned around and ran back to the dining room and grabbed a swatch of pink polka-dot fabric and a black Sharpie from a jar.

Aunt Lulu raised her eyebrows as Zoey skipped back with the swatch in her hand.

"For her to sign," Zoey explained. "I had this idea that maybe if I could get a bunch of designers' autographs, I could make a quilt or something."

Aunt Lulu put her arm across Zoey's shoulders and ushered her out the door. "You continue to amaze me, Zo. If I were half as creative as you, I could turn my little interior design business into a multimedia empire, I bet."

"And hire a whole staff to walk Draper?" asked Zoey.

"Exactly!" Aunt Lulu said.

By the time they picked up Priti and got to the fabric store, it was nearly six o'clock. But Zoey was happy to discover that the line to get books signed wasn't a mile long after all.

"See," said Aunt Lulu. "I told you. We're absolutely fine."

"Oh look! There she is!" said Priti, pointing to a woman at a table, set up in the middle of the store, piled high with books.

"Cecily Chen!" Zoey squealed under her breath. She would have known her anywhere. The signature glasses. The long black hair with a streak of pink.

"Come on!" She grabbed Priti's hand, and they joined the line and waited impatiently for it to move.

"I'm so glad you told me about this," said Priti.

"Thanks for coming," Zoey said. "Too bad Kate had her soccer thing. And too bad Libby had her aunt here. You know, I'm pretty sure she actually has a Cecily Chen shirt."

"Really?" asked Priti.

Zoey nodded. "Yeah, from the spring line, I think. I saw one just like it in *Très Chic*."

Priti pulled in her chin, impressed.

"I know," Zoey said. "It's funny. Just when you think she's not into fashion, she shows up in something really new and cool . . . Ooh!" She grabbed on to Priti's sleeve. "We're next! Go, go, go!"

They stepped up to the table, and Cecily Chen smiled up at them.

"Zoey!" Jan was sitting beside the designer, keeping track of the books that were sold. Her own long black hair was up in a loose, high bun.

The store owner turned to the designer. "Oh,

Cecily, you have to meet my newest Stitch in Time wunderkind, Zoey Webber," she declared. "Zoey, so glad that you could come and bring a friend!"

Cecily Chen held out her hand to shake Zoey's. "Wow, that's quite an introduction. It's nice to meet you," she told Zoey.

"It's nice to meet *you*, Ms. Chen!" Zoey gushed. "I'm a big, huge, ginormous fan! And I can't wait to read your book! Your fall line is amazing, by the way. I watched the whole show online. I just love how you took the minimal thing you did in the spring and just kind of turned it inside out."

"Thanks!" the designer said with a smile that was both pleased and a little surprised. "That was exactly what I was trying to do . . ." She leaned over, closer to Jan. "Wow, she gets a lot more than some fashion editors I know."

"Oh, she knows her stuff," said Jan. "And her sewing skills are coming right along. You better watch out. She'll be your competition one day. Mark my words."

Cecily Chen turned back to Zoey, adjusting her glasses as she did. "That's pretty big praise, I must say. Don't tell me you made that great outfit you're wearing." She grinned.

"Oh, she definitely made it!" said Priti before Zoey could reply. "She designs clothes and sews them *all* the time. You should check out her blog!" she added. Then she stuck out her hand. "Hi! I'm Priti, by the way. I don't sew . . . but I'm a big fan!"

"You know, she's right, Cecily!" Jan spoke up. "You should definitely check out the blog. It's called Sew Zoey, and you'd just love it. Plus, she has nice things to say about A Stitch in Time." She winked at Zoey, then she suddenly noticed the stalled line. "Oops! Better keep things moving! We've got a lot of books to sign!"

"Of course!" Cecily held up her pen and clicked it as Zoey and Priti gave her their books.

"Oh! Could you sign this, too? Please?" Zoey asked, pulling out her fabric swatch from her bag. She unfolded it and handed it to the designer, along with the Sharpie she'd brought.

"Well, this is a new one! I like it!" Cecily Chen said, enthusiastically signing her name.

Zoey and Priti moved away from the table a few

moments later, with the autographed fabric and two signed books.

Priti eagerly read what the designer had written: "'To Priti, a great friend—Thanks for being a great fan, too!' So cool!" she exclaimed, turning to Zoey. "What does yours say?"

Zoey opened her book to the title page, where Cecily Chen's bold, elegant handwriting swept across the bottom half. "'To Zoey, my fellow designer, I hope you like this book! And I hope you'll write one too one day—and sign it for me, of course!'"

"Did she really write that?" demanded Priti, peeking over Zoey's shoulder. "Oh my gosh! She's so nice! And she's right! You should write a book! Don't you think?"

Zoey rolled her eyes and smiled over her shoulder back at Priti. "Are you kidding? I can barely write a blog!"

---------- CHAPTER 3 ----------

All About Ikat

Attention! Run, do not walk, to your local bookstore and buy Cecily Chen's book today! I got home last night and started reading and couldn't put it down.

I still can't believe I actually met her—and that she complimented my outfit too! Here's a sketch of what I wore. Remember this bubble skirt I made out of T-shirt material? Well, check it out. . . . I thought I'd pair it with this ikat top I made the other day. (BTW, look out for some Cecily Chen ikat in the near future . . . and remember you heard it here first!) Plus my signature zigzag bangle and the cutest cowboy boots I (literally!) stumbled upon at the thrift store last week (hence the polka-dot bandage I'm wearing on my knee).

But now it's Monday morning and time to get back to reality. Same old, same old, except for one thing . . . I'm wearing that football jersey dress to school today! I've already decided I'm going to tackle anyone who teases me about it. Just kidding! ☺ But that would be funny, wouldn't it? Stay tuned, sports fans . . .

"Awesome dress."

"Thanks." Zoey looked up from her desk in social studies, smiling. She was starting to get used to people complimenting her clothes.

Huh?

Lorenzo Romy?

What Zoey totally *wasn't* used to was getting

compliments from him. In fact, she was pretty sure he hadn't said ten words to her since their school play in fifth grade. She really didn't know a lot about him, just that he hung out with all the jocks. And, well, looking at him, he did have kind of nice eyes . . . and a cute way of smiling with one side of his face. It was probably the eyes and the smile, she figured, that was suddenly making her feel kind of strange. Strange and slightly dumb—as in she couldn't think of what to say.

"Big fan?" He kept grinning.

"Fan?" she repeated. She knew that was the wrong answer, but it was all she had right then.

"ESU. Go, Eagles." He did a fist pump. "Too bad about last week's game, huh? My parents both went there, and I'm definitely going. You too?"

"Oh . . ." Zoey got it now. Her dress. The colors. Of course. "My dad works there," she explained, shrugging. "But I don't really—"

"No way. That's awesome," he interrupted. "What does he do?"

"He's a physical therapist. . . . He works with the athletes and—"

"Wow. Really? Cool!"

Zoey nodded. Kind of, she guessed. She'd never given it that much thought.

"So where'd you get it?" he asked.

"What?" She looked down. "My dress?"

"Yeah. Did you buy it on campus?"

"No . . . actually . . . I made it," she said.

"You *made* it? Are you serious? Like, with a sewing machine?" he asked, impressed.

She knew she was smiling. She was afraid she was a little red, too.

"Wow, that's awesome!" he went on. "You should make more and take them to games or something. You could probably sell a ton!"

Zoey was positive she was red now. But she didn't even care. Selling her own clothes was her dream. She wondered if Lorenzo had any idea . . .

"Good morning, students." Mr. Dunn, their social studies teacher, suddenly closed the classroom door with a solid *thwam*. "We have a lot to cover this morning, so please take your seats. *Ah-hem*. Mr. Romy-O. Yes, I'm talking to you. Sit down."

Lorenzo shrugged, shifting his backpack, and turned to walk away. Zoey watched him . . . then opened her notebook . . . then cut her eyes to watch him again. Boys were not something she usually worried about very much. Not on purpose . . . That was just how it was. She'd always left crushes and flirting to girls in her class like Ivy Wallace, who seemed to live for that kind of stuff. But then again, boys had never shown her a lot of interest—or used the word "awesome" to her face. She couldn't help wondering if it meant something. And was that why she was feeling this funny way? It was like someone (a.k.a. Lorenzo Romy) had flipped a switch and lit up a room inside her that had, until then, been dark. It was weird, but in a good way . . . and it made listening to Mr. Dunn very hard.

By lunch Zoey's funny feeling had faded a little, but it hadn't completely gone away. She wondered if her friends could tell there was something different about her when they met at their usual table to eat.

"Yuck." Kate looked down at her tray and glumly picked up her spork. "Macaroni and cheese can be so good. Why does the school's version have to be so bad? I wish I'd looked at the menu. I totally would have brought my lunch."

Priti peeked into her brown bag. "I'll trade you," she offered. "My mom packed samosas . . . *again*."

"Deal!" Kate instantly slid her tray over and seized Priti's bag. "These are so good, Priti! Why don't you want them?" She pulled one out, peeled off its foil wrapper, took a bite, and closed her eyes.

Priti shrugged. "What can I say? Even delicious things get old when you have them every day." She took a bite of Kate's mac and cheese. "Yeah, it's not so great, is it? Hey, look!" She pointed to Zoey, holding some of the cheesy macaroni on her spork. "It matches Zoey's dress. What are you having?" she asked, nodding to Zoey's unopened bag.

"Hmm?" Zoey tore her eyes away from Lorenzo, who had just taken a seat across the cafeteria at a table full of guys. She'd been watching him ever since she noticed him striding up to the hot-lunch line.

Priti changed the question. "Zoey, what are you staring at?" she asked.

"What? Nothing," Zoey said. She picked up her brown bag and pulled out a sandwich that she'd made herself that morning.

"Nutella and banana?" Kate asked.

Zoey grinned and nodded. "What else? Oh hey, Libby!" She waved to their new friend, who was getting there late, as usual, thanks to Mr. Dunn. Libby had the misfortune of having his class right before lunch. Not only did he like to keep talking after the bell rang, his room was about as far from the cafeteria as possible.

"Hey!" Libby sat down, slightly breathless, and shared a smile. "Cute dress!" she told Zoey.

"Thanks!" Zoey said.

Kate raised a samosa. "My idea! I'm Zoey's muse today!"

"Oh, the football game!" said Libby. "Those are the ESU colors—I love it!" She patted the sleeve.

"Have you gotten a lot of comments?" asked Kate.

Zoey bit her lip. Her eyes darted back to Lorenzo's table. "Well . . . I got an 'awesome' this morning," she said.

"Oh yeah? From who?"

"Lo—" Zoey said—almost. She cleared her throat and tried again. "Lorenzo Romy. You guys know him . . . right?"

"Oh yeah." Kate nodded. "He's on the swim team. He's a good backstroker. And a *really* good soccer player, too," she said.

"Yeah . . . he seems nice," said Zoey, trying to sound casual and as if she hadn't been thinking about him all day. "Do you . . ."

"What?" said Priti, waiting.

"Do we what?" Kate wondered too.

Zoey bit her lip. *Good question,* she thought. *I don't know. . . .*

Did they think he was cute? Did they think he might like her? What exactly did she want to know?

Nothing. She wanted to know nothing, she decided. And she knew she wanted to change the subject—fast.

"Ooh, nice bracelets," she said, suddenly noticing pretty new ones dangling from Libby's wrists.

They were very delicate—like Libby—and made out of different-colored silk cords. Pink, yellow, green, blue, orange, and bright cherry red. Each had a single long, thin gold bead and was bound with a neat sliding knot.

"Oh, thanks." Libby smiled.

"Where'd you get them?" Zoey had to ask.

Libby shrugged and blushed a little. "My aunt gave them to me."

Wow . . . Zoey couldn't help glancing at Kate and Priti, who were clearly thinking the same thing. Who was this relative! There hadn't been a single "That's great! Where'd you get what you're wearing, Libby?" question yet that hadn't been answered that same way.

"The aunt who visited you this weekend?" Zoey asked.

Libby nodded. "Uh-huh. She doesn't have her own kids, so she kind of spoils me. You know how that is."

Zoey sure did. She thought about her own aunt Lulu, who was always doing things for her. She let Zoey hang out at her house in the summer and paid her way too much to walk her dog. And Zoey had Aunt Lulu to thank for most of her fabric and patterns, as well as for teaching her to sew.

Gifts of beautiful designer clothes and jewelry, though . . . ? Mmm, not so much.

"Where does she get it all? Do you know?" asked Zoey.

"Uh, work, pretty much," Libby said.

Zoey's eyes got big. Her work? Really? *That's* how she got all this fabulous stuff? "What kind of amazing job does she have?" Zoey had to know.

Libby looked down at her tray. "She's a buyer," she explained.

"A buyer?" Kate's nose wrinkled.

"For H. Cashin's. The department store? She picks out stuff from designers for the store to sell."

"No way!" Zoey exclaimed. *H. Cashin's? Really?* That was a huge, world-famous store! She couldn't believe that Libby hadn't told them yet. Never said a word. If *her* aunt had been a buyer for H. Cashin's, Zoey would have alerted the whole universe!

And what a great job! thought Zoey. Next to being a fashion designer, or maybe a stylist, it seemed like something she'd *love* to do.

"Does she like it?" she asked Libby eagerly. "I'd

love to meet her. . . . Is she coming back soon?"

Libby suddenly got quiet. She scooped some mac and cheese onto her spork. "No. Probably not," she said. "She's really busy with work."

"Too bad," said Zoey. She was dying to ask some more questions, but she kept them to herself. She didn't know why, but Libby didn't seem to want to keep talking about her aunt. . . .

"Well, tell your aunt that anything she doesn't think is right for you, she can send this way!" Priti declared.

Zoey saw a frown flick across Libby's forehead. "Of course, she's just kidding!" Zoey quickly said.

"I am?" Priti said, then she giggled. Zoey and Kate did too.

Libby seemed to try to laugh, but Zoey was pretty sure a mysterious frown was still there, somewhere, underneath.

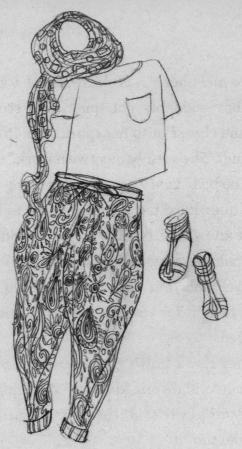

-------------- CHAPTER 4 ----------

Closet Safari Day!

Talk about happy surprises! My football jersey dress? Big, huge, surprisingly AWESOME success! So great that I was tempted to wear it again! (LOL! Just kidding, of course. I think you probably know me well enough by now to know that nothing but fashion armageddon could make me wear an outfit two times in a row. ☺) Not that I haven't been sewing. It's just I've been working on something else. I'm afraid I can't tell you what, though. (It's a top-secret surprise for a friend!)

So what *am* I wearing today? Nothing I made myself, actually. Today's what I like to call Closet Safari Day. I started with some paisley harem pants, à la the eighties, and which I've always had a love-hate relationship with. (Yes, the pants were my mom's. And yes, they are a little big. But that's never stopped me before, and it feels like going to school in pajamas!) I paired them with sandals, even though I'll have to change them for gym. Oh! And I DID make part of this outfit. The scarf! Kind of. I had all these small silky scarves from who knows where—and I cut them into squares and sewed them together to make one superlong, crazy one. My aunt Lulu called it my "scarf of many colors" when she saw it. It's pretty awesome, don't you think? I wonder if anyone else will think it's awesome today . . . ?

"Okay, let's see 'em!"

Zoey grabbed Kate on Tuesday morning as soon

as she got on the bus. Kate fell in the seat with a warm, wide smile. But it was also tightly shut.

"*Kate*," Zoey groaned teasingly . . . until Kate finally opened up.

"Oh my gosh!" She gasped. Kate's teeth!

Zoey had forgotten what Kate looked like, she realized, before she had a robot smile. No more braces didn't just change the way her mouth looked, it changed the look of her whole face! She looked so . . . pretty. Not that Kate hadn't before. But somehow it was different. Now she looked like someone people might stare at as she walked by.

Zoey watched Kate run her tongue back and forth over her top row of newly naked teeth.

"It feels so weird!" Kate told her.

"Like how?" Zoey asked.

Kate checked her teeth with her tongue again. "Like they're fake or something. And they're so slippery. It's like they're covered with wax. Ugh! I can't stop feeling them! Do I look like a crazy person?" she asked.

Zoey laughed. "No, you look amazing!" And really, Kate totally did.

Zoey spun around and peered over the back of the seat at little Jacob Straub. He was staring intently at his phone and swiping his finger away at the screen.

"Jacob," she said. "Jacob?"

"Hmm?" he answered without looking up.

"Check it out." Zoey put her arm across Kate's shoulders. "Smile, Kate," she said. "Jacob, have you seen Kate without her braces yet? Doesn't she look great?"

He sighed and looked up finally—but Kate had already shrunk down.

"Sit down, you!" said Kate, pulling Zoey down beside her and shaking her head. She rolled her eyes, smiling. "Promise me something."

"Anything," said Zoey. "What?"

"Promise me you that you won't make a big deal about my getting my braces off when we get to school."

Zoey nodded. She could tell Kate was serious. She had raised her I-mean-business eyebrows.

"I'll do my best . . . ," said Zoey, shrugging. Then she squeezed Kate's hand and grinned. "No, really, I promise. I get it. It's not a big deal at all."

"Good! So what's in the bag?" Kate asked, glancing down at the plastic shopping bag next to Zoey's feet. The shopping bag that held the surprise Zoey and Priti had planned for Kate!

"This? Oh, nothing," Zoey said quickly, moving her legs to cover the bag. "Stuff . . . you know . . ." She smiled innocently. "No big deal at all!"

"*Kate!*"

Kate hadn't even left the lunch line before Priti was shouting her name.

"Kate! I hardly recognize you! You look amazing!" she cried, running up. "Seriously! I am *so* jealous. I can't wait till my braces come off now!"

Priti hugged Kate as best she could around Kate's loaded tray. As Priti did, she looked over Kate's shoulder at Zoey. *Do you have the bag?* she mouthed.

Zoey nodded and held up the shopping bag, and Priti released Kate with a squeal.

Zoey and Priti had met quickly between English and gym to assemble Kate's surprise. They'd decided that lunch was the best time to give it to her, considering what was inside.

"Kate!" said Priti. "Why are you keeping your mouth closed? You've got to smile and show off those pearly whites!"

Kate, meanwhile, had shrunk about two inches and turned a bright shade of pink. She took a deep breath and marched toward their usual table, eyes down and shaking her head.

Priti turned to Zoey. "What did I do?"

"Too much attention, I think," said Zoey. "You know how Kate is. She likes to be in the background, *not* the star of the show."

"I know," said Priti. "But I can't help it! She looks so pretty, don't you think?"

Zoey nodded. "Yeah! *So* pretty! I told her, too. And don't think she really minds it so much from you or from me. But after four periods of people staring at her, she's kind of overwhelmed, you know? You haven't had a class with her yet, but you should have seen the kids in English. It was like she'd suddenly come back from getting a total face transplant."

Zoey had been faithful in keeping her promise to Kate all morning long. She hadn't said another word about how great Kate looked or pointed out her perfect smile to anyone else. But the instant they walked through the front doors of school, Kate's teeth advertised themselves.

It started with Ms. Austen, their new principal, who greeted the students every day.

"Good morning, Zoey . . . Kate," she said warmly, as always.

"Good morning, Ms. Austen," they replied. They both smiled as they passed by her, then all of a sudden the principal's eyes got wide.

Honestly, Zoey thought at first Ms. Austen had noticed her harem pants and was about to exclaim that she once had some just like them. But it was Kate's smile the principal honed in on.

"You got your braces off, Kate. Congratulations. You look lovely!" she remarked.

Kate turned a little pink but was also clearly pleased. But that, it turned out, was just the beginning. Before they knew it, students were stopping to talk to Kate as she hurried down the hall.

"You got your braces off!"

"You look great, Kate!"

"Hello, gorgeous!" one boy even said.

Zoey turned to stare as he walked away. "Kate! Did you hear what he said?"

Kate linked her arm with Zoey's and kept going. "That's Kevin Malouf," she told Zoey, impatiently shaking her head. "He was on my Little League team for two years. He's just teasing. . . ."

Zoey wasn't so sure, though. He looked pretty serious. So did a lot of other boys that suddenly paused by Kate's locker to "chat."

She could tell Kate felt self-conscious and was longing for all the attention to stop. So then why, Zoey suddenly wondered, was she starting to feel—what *was* it? Could it be?—jealous of her best friend?

It was just the teeniest, *tiniest* feeling, but it was there, like a snag in an otherwise perfectly great pair of tights. It wasn't as if Zoey didn't get attention herself these days, but it was for her clothes, and that felt very different from getting attention for her looks.

Zoey was just glad the feeling subsided and that by lunchtime it was gone. Instead, she was focused on giving Kate her one-of-a-kind surprise.

"Come on!" she told Priti, nodding toward their lunch table. "What are we waiting for? Hurry up!"

They sat down just as Kate was coming out of the lunch line, fielding a compliment from the lunch lady by trying to smile with her mouth closed. Zoey and Priti watched from afar as Kate picked up her lunch tray and, flustered, walked right into Ivy Wallace and Bree Sharpe.

"Hey, watch it, Brace Face!" Ivy snapped. She gave a pointed look to Bree.

"Yeah," added Bree. "Looks like you need glasses, too."

Kate didn't say a word. She just smiled for real this time, teeth and all.

"Oh, uh, um," Ivy stuttered, then paused for what seemed like an eternity. "Big deal. You got your braces off. I didn't even have to have braces."

"Yeah, Ivy's teeth are perfect," Bree agreed on cue, but her cheeks turned red as she said it.

Kate shrugged it off and ignored them, walking

proudly to the table where Zoey and Priti were sitting and watching in awe.

"Nicely done!" Priti said, giving Kate a high five.

"Thanks," Kate replied, smiling a little.

Just then, Libby arrived and sat down.

"Oh good!" said Zoey. "You're just in time!"

"For what?" Libby and Kate both asked.

Zoey shared a smile with Priti. "Well, as you know, this is a very big day. . . ."

"Right!" Libby turned to Kate. "You got your braces off! How does it feel?"

Kate smiled shyly, half-showing her perfect teeth, and shrugged again. "Good," she answered self-consciously. "Weird . . . but good, I guess."

"Well, you look great," said Libby, smiling back.

"I know!" said Priti. "That's just what I said!"

"Anyway . . ." Zoey cleared her throat. "After two long, gummy-bear-free years, we thought this was the best way to say 'bye-bye, braces!'"

With that, Zoey lifted her shopping bag onto her lap and pulled out the oversized lunch bag she'd sewn, setting it down with a *thump* on the table in front of Kate's lunch tray.

"Go ahead! Open it!" Zoey said.

"You guys!" Kate couldn't even hope to hide her teeth then, her smile was so huge. She reached for the bag. "I love it! It's so cute!"

Then she saw what was inside, and her mouth formed a giant O. She pulled out an apple, a jar of peanut butter, a box of toffee-covered popcorn, three packs of bubble gum, and chocolate chews.

"*Yes!* I missed these so much!" she exclaimed. Then she dug back into the bag. "Oh wow! Swedish Fish! You guys! Yum! And gummy frogs! And worms!"

Finally, Kate pulled out a tube-shaped object wrapped in shiny foil. "Is this what I think it is?" she asked.

Priti nodded. "If you're thinking corn on the cob," she said, "then yes, I think it is!"

Kate unwrapped it and took a bite. "Yum," she said, licking her lips. "It's even good cold."

"Did the butter get hard?" asked Zoey.

"A little. But who cares!" Kate grinned. She picked up the bag of gummy frogs and passed it around. "Here, you guys, have some!"

"Thanks!" Libby took one.

Zoey did as well.

Priti, though, had to sigh and shake her head sadly. "I forgot how much torture this would be for *me*," she said, settling for a spoonful of applesauce.

Kate put her arm across Priti's shoulders. "Poor Priti," she said. "Sure you don't want one anyway?"

Priti thought about it for a second, then shook her head again. "Better not. I don't want to run around school with braces full of green goo. But promise me you'll remember to do this when *my* braces come off. Okay?"

"Are you kidding?" said Zoey. "I've already got the bag made!"

"Just look out," said Kate, licking her fingers, "and know that getting your braces off has its downside, too."

"What do you mean?" Priti asked.

"Remember how people stared at you when you got them on?"

Priti shrugged. "Yeah, I guess."

"Well, it's even worse when you get them off," Kate declared.

"Oh, don't worry," said Priti. "That's not going to bother me. When have I ever minded extra attention? Hmm?"

"She has a good point," said Zoey.

"I guess you're right," Kate agreed. "Still, I don't get why everyone has to make such a big deal about me. Except for my mouth, I'm exactly the same."

"Hey, Kate!"

The whole table looked up to see a group of boys clustered like pigeons around Kate's chair, though Lorenzo Romy was the only one who Zoey could focus on at first.

"Oh, hi. What's up?" Kate smiled—with her lips securely closed.

"Hey. So what are you doing tomorrow?" asked Alec Burns, the tallest one.

"Tomorrow? Oh right," said Kate. "We have the day off. I almost forgot."

Zoey had too. The first teacher conference day of the year. They hadn't made any plans for it at all, though Zoey did have a skirt she wanted to hem.

"Are we doing anything?" Kate looked around the table.

"Toronto. Remember?" Priti said. It was her grandparents' fiftieth anniversary, and there was going to be a huge party where they lived. Her whole family from all over the world was coming, and they had days of activities planned, which meant that even though they had Wednesday off, Priti would miss school through to the weekend.

"I'm visiting my grandparents too," said Libby. "But they just live in the nursing home here in town. My mom and I are taking them to lunch."

"I'm free," Zoey said, shrugging, as if boys asked what she was doing every day. She didn't even realize she was staring right at Lorenzo until his eyes caught her and it was too late.

"Oh no, that's okay," said Alec. "We just need Kate."

Oh . . . Zoey instantly bent down her head. She bit the head off a gummy frog. She forgot all about the chewing part, though, and let it sink to the back of her throat. She could feel her cheeks starting to burn. Her neck was heating up too. She lowered her head even farther, hoping she didn't explode.

"Why me?" she heard Kate ask.

"'Cause you're on the soccer team," Lorenzo explained.

"Yeah, we had this idea," said another boy, Bobby. "Mapleton soccer tournament. Boys team against girls. One o'clock, out on the field."

"You in, Kate?" asked Lorenzo.

Zoey peeked back up at him, at last. He wasn't looking at her anymore.

"Are you kidding?" said Kate. Her smile widened. "You all are so going down!"

"Hey! Did you get your braces off?" Lorenzo asked, suddenly leaning closer.

Kate's lips automatically closed.

"I told you she did," Alec said.

"You look awesome, Kate!" Lorenzo declared.

Kate glanced down and mumbled, "Thanks" as the other boys chimed in to agree.

That's when Zoey felt a lump in her throat. Was it a gummy frog head stuck on the way down? Or was it her heart breaking as she remembered how special she felt when Lorenzo told her she was awesome? Whatever it was, it hurt.

Lorenzo, meanwhile, leaned over Kate even

farther. "Where'd you get all the candy?" he asked.

"Excuse me. From my friends," Kate said, playfully pushing him back.

"Ooh! Can we have some?" he asked her.

"Please!" Alec begged.

Kate smiled and rolled her eyes. "Here." She handed them a bag of gummy worms.

"Thanks, Kate!" they yelled, attacking it.

"Yeah, thanks, Kate!" said Lorenzo. "You rock!"

"Look! Check it out!" shouted Bobby, dangling a green candy from his nose.

With that, they trooped off, stuffing their faces, and Zoey finally raised her head. There were reasons she didn't worry about boys too much, and that was definitely one.

She waited for Kate to say something like "*Gross! Sorry, girls!*" or "*Boys. They never change.*"

But instead she was actually smiling at them and returning Lorenzo's wave.

Boys never change, thought Zoey.

But what about Kate?

------------ CHAPTER 5 ----------

All Smiles? Brace Yourself.

First of all, thanks for all the awesome comments on my scarf today, Sew Zoey readers. I'm glad you liked it . . . because no one at school noticed it, really. That kind of surprised me, since it's hard to miss! Then again, it's hard to compete with the other big news from yesterday. There's a hint in the sketch. See the bracket pattern? Can you tell I have braces on the brain?

My best friend Kate got her braces off and has the most perfect pearly whites! Honestly, Kate looks amazing. My aunt Lulu's right: Smiles really are the best accessories. With that in mind, I started thinking about branching out into an accessory line, as so many designers do. Presenting the Sew Zoey Smile Line . . . (Toothbrushes not included. Braces optional! ☺)

Zoey finished typing and clicked publish and tried to tell herself not to mope. So what if Lorenzo didn't say one word to her all day at school? And so what if he stared at Kate? She should never have gotten so carried away by one dumb "awesome." After all, it was just a word.

I will not be jealous, she told herself. But that was easier said than done. Just when Zoey thought she'd chased the feeling away, it would sneak back up on her.

She checked her e-mail halfheartedly, just looking for something to do. That's when she noticed a new one and nearly collapsed onto her keyboard.

The sender was Cecily@CChen.com.

Cecily Chen was writing to *her*!

Zoey quickly opened the e-mail and read it. And when she was done, she read it again.

Dear Zoey,

It was so nice to meet you at my book signing. Thank you again for coming with your friend! And thank you for telling me about your blog. I finally got home and had a chance to read it, and I absolutely love it! Really! I wish I had half the ideas you have when I was your age. Even now, I could see several of your designs on the runway in New York. In fact, do you know that one of my favorite fabric companies, Avalon, has an amateur design and sewing contest in celebration of their one hundredth birthday going on right now? Most of the entrants will be adults, but I checked, and there are no age requirements, and I think you should go for it!

I'm attaching a link to the contest website, in case you're interested—which I hope you are! Let me know what you decide, but you have to do it fast! The deadline is coming up very soon. In the meantime, I plan to keep enjoying your blog. It's the perfect thing to read as I work on a brand-new tween line for the mass market that will be coming out soon!

    Thanks for inspiring me!

Your friend in fashion,

    Cecily

PS Please tell Jan hello from me the next time you see her!

Zoey immediately clicked on the contest link and opened the website and read through the contest rules. She couldn't see anything about being eighteen or any age to enter—just that the design had to be original, and "one hundred percent designed and sewn by you!" The grand prize winner, she read, would have their garment reproduced—in the company's fabric—and that wasn't all. It would be sold throughout the country next spring . . . in H. Cashin's department stores!

Cecily Chen was right. It was an amazing opportunity, which Zoey would be insane to miss. But she was also right that the deadline was soon—as in photos of the garments, made and on real, live models, had to be submitted by the end of that weekend!

The design part didn't worry Zoey so much. That came easily to her, and she could already think of a few dresses from her sketchbook that would be perfect to work from. It was the *sewing* part that made Zoey chew the inside of her cheek. It wouldn't be like following a pattern. Zoey would have to make that up too . . . something she'd tried a couple of times but was still figuring out how to do. Luckily she had a trusty helper: Marie Antoinette. That was what she'd named the adjustable dress form that her aunt Lulu had given her. At the moment, Marie wasn't wearing much, except for a gorilla mask on her headless neck. Marcus had tossed it there as a joke, but Zoey had decided to keep it for a while because it made her laugh.

Zoey looked at the Year of Fashion calendar on her bedroom wall. She had five days to make something—minus all the time she was in school. Was it even possible? No, wait! She had tomorrow off. That made all the difference in the world!

Zoey went back into her e-mail and wrote a reply to Cecily Chen as fast as she could.

Dear Cecily,
Thank you so much for your e-mail and for liking my blog! And thank you for telling me about the sewing contest. I had no idea it was going on! I don't know if I can design and sew a winner by the deadline . . . but I'm definitely going to try!
Thanks again!
Your friend in fashion too!
Zoey
PS I'll be sure to tell Jan you say hi the next time I see her—which, thanks to this contest, will be very, very soon!

"Guys! Guess what!"

Zoey ran down to the family room, where her dad and Marcus were watching what looked like the very same football highlights they'd sat and watched the night before.

"What's up?" Her dad turned to her, grinning. "Hey, shouldn't you be ready for bed?"

"No school tomorrow. Remember?" said Zoey, hurrying on to her big news. "So, guess what? There's this sewing contest for Avalon Fabrics. You have to design and sew a dress for their one hundredth anniversary. And guess what the grand prize is?"

Her dad shrugged.

"They make your dress and they actually *sell* it. At H. Cashin's! How great is that?!"

"They sell one dress?" Marcus asked. He was lying on the sofa and didn't look away from the TV screen.

"*No,*" said Zoey. "They make a lot! Hundreds! Enough to sell in all their stores!"

"Wow," said Marcus, finally looking at Zoey. "That's cool, Zo. Any chance H. Cashin's is having a drumming contest too?"

"Ha-ha," Zoey said, leaning over him. "Very funny."

Zoey's dad raised an eyebrow. "To think, my brilliant daughter's clothes are going to be in a fancy department store."

"Hold on a sec, Dad." Zoey laughed. "I haven't

won it yet! And the deadline's on Sunday."

"*This* Sunday?" her dad asked. He looked at Zoey. Then at Marcus. Then, doubtfully, at his watch.

Marcus pointed a mischievous finger at Zoey. "Looks like someone's going to need some energy juice, Dad," he joked.

Zoey shook her head and grabbed her stomach. "Oh no. I don't think so!"

She ran back to her room to get started on a sketch. She was feeling pretty great—awesome, actually. And then she remembered Lorenzo. She wondered who he thought was the most awesome. Was it Kate?

I can't be jealous of Kate, Zoey thought. *She's my best friend!* Zoey forced herself to snap out of it, more grateful than ever to have a sewing project to distract her.

The next morning Zoey woke up later than usual. She'd stayed up way too late working on her design for the contest. Her dad came into her room on his way to work.

"Rise and shine! I'm off," he said.

"Huh?" Zoey glanced at her clock. "Eight thirty, *already*?" She groaned.

He chuckled and kissed her lightly on the top of her tousled head. "There's cereal for breakfast. Marcus does have school, you know, so he's already gone. But Aunt Lulu said she'd check in on you. Do you have much homework to get done?"

Zoey groggily shook her head. "No . . . thank goodness," she said. Then she yawned and stretched and rolled over and pointed to the open sketchbook by her bed. "I have that contest to work on, remember? What do you think of these sketches?"

Her dad picked up the book and studied it for a second with the faintest of frowns. "Ah!" He grinned and flipped it over. "That's much better," he joked.

"You're hilarious, Dad," said Zoey as she smiled and sat up. "Seriously. What do you think?"

He nodded. "I think these are really great, hon. They *all* look like winners to me." He handed the book back to her. "Which one do you think you're going to pick?"

"I don't know. . . ." She rubbed her eyes. "That's my job for today, I guess."

CHAPTER 6

Make a Wish

News! Big news! News so humongous you have to sit down! Okay, I guess there's a good chance you're already sitting while you read this, so . . . hold on to your hats! I'm entering Avalon Fabrics' Break-Out Designer contest! It's their one hundredth anniversary, and the grand prize winner gets to have their dress produced and sold at H. Cashin's department stores nationwide!!! Did I mention that H. Cashin's is my happy place? When I go there I feel like I'm walking through a fashion magazine. All of which means I really, really, really want to win!

There is a catch. I haven't quite come up with an entry yet—and it has to be sewn and photographed by THIS SUNDAY NIGHT! But, hey! They do it in even less time every week on *Fashion Showdown*, right? So why can't I?

Maybe because I keep wasting time getting carried away with sketching ideas. As soon as I read that the contest was to celebrate Avalon's birthday, I started to think about birthday cakes! The "birthday cake dress" would be pretty in pink, with fabric twisted to look like icing, and layers of ruffles. So pretty, right? And then I started thinking about cupcakes . . . and how accordion pleats would make the skirt look just like a cupcake wrapper and the top could look like swirls of frosting covered in sprinkle-shaped beads. Or maybe I could make a dress covered with one hundred twinkly lights to stand in for birthday candles? Not sure that one would work, but it's so much fun to imagine. So, here's the one-hundred-twinkly-light question: I think they're sweet (pun intended), but would anyone shopping at H. Cashin's actually wear these? Does it matter? For now, it's back to the drawing board. Wish me luck.

Zoey spent the whole morning sketching . . . and sketching some more. By the time Aunt Lulu stopped by the house around noon, Zoey had used up three mechanical pencils and every scrap of paper in her room. She laid out a dozen designs for Aunt Lulu to look at as soon as she walked through the door.

"Well, what are we waiting for?" asked Aunt Lulu after Zoey outlined how the contest would work. "Sounds to me like we need to take a trip to A Stitch in Time, don't you think?"

She was right, of course. Designing the dress was just the beginning. Zoey had to sew it too.

"But I can't get fabric till I know what I'm making," Zoey explained to her.

"Oh, I don't know," Aunt Lulu replied. "You're

very close, I think, and I wonder if seeing what fabric you have to choose from—in person—might help you narrow your ideas down even more. You never know. Plus, I was kind of feeling Yo-Yum for lunch, and it's right next door, you know."

Zoey ran to find her bag. "You're right! What *are* we waiting for?"

Aunt Lulu was great in so many ways that it was impossible to count. But way up there on the list was definitely her willingness to consider frozen yogurt—even chocolate—a wholesome and nutritious, well-balanced, anytime meal.

They drove to the yogurt shop, where Zoey ordered a large chocolate and pomegranate swirl. She topped it with coconut and raspberries and a sprinkle of Cap'n Crunch. Her recyclable bowl was nearly as clean as new by the time she was done.

"Thanks! That hit the spot," she told Aunt Lulu as they made their way next door.

"Well, it's about time you got here!" Jan called as soon as they walked into her store. "That contest dress of yours sure isn't going to make itself!"

Zoey laughed. Sometimes she forgot that what

she wrote on her blog was actually read.

"Don't remind me," Zoey replied. "And, honestly, I'm still not sure what I'm doing yet, but we thought it might help to come in and look around."

"Be my guest," said Jan. "Most of my Avalon fabric is back with the silks. But if you have any trouble finding what you want, just holler, do you hear?"

"Thanks!" Zoey said just as her phone went off.

She pulled it out from deep in her bag. It was a text from Kate: **Where r u?** it said.

Zoey frowned . . . and thought . . . and winced.

Ugh! Right. Kate's boy-girl soccer game. After school the day before, Kate has asked her to come and watch. "Sure," Zoey had told her. But then she got Cecily Chen's e-mail . . . and she completely forgot. She felt awful. Oh, but Kate would understand. She was probably just texting to be nice, anyway.

Sorry! she quickly texted back. **Did u read my blog? Big sewing contest! Dress due Sunday! Good luck and lmk the score!**

She hit send and set her course for the Avalon aisle. Soon she was in her own personal heaven, looking through bolts and bolts of beautiful fabric.

The next morning Zoey daydreamed about her Avalon designs while she waited for the bus to arrive at Kate's stop.

"Hey!" Zoey smiled at Kate as climbed on.

"Hi," said Kate, sinking into the seat across the aisle.

"So, how was the game?"

"Good," said Kate.

"You guys won?"

"Uh-huh. Four to two."

"Did you score?" Zoey asked.

Kate nodded matter-of-factly. "Two."

"That's great!" Zoey grinned and waited for more details . . . but Kate seemed ready to move on.

"So . . . how's your contest thing coming?" she asked.

"Ugh!" Zoey groaned. "It's so much work. I haven't even started sewing yet—or decided on my final design."

"It's due this weekend?"

"Yeah." Zoey nodded. "Sunday night. By then I have to have it finished and send in a picture of somebody *in* it. I guess since they're actually going to *sell* the winning piece, they want to make sure it can really be worn."

Kate grinned. "Marie Antoinette's not good enough?"

Zoey smiled back. "Apparently not. But we won't tell her. And don't worry . . . I'm not going to ask *you*," she assured Kate. "You're totally off the hook. I actually thought I'd ask Libby, since Priti's away, and she did so great modeling in the school fashion show for me."

"Oh . . . that makes sense," said Kate softly, leaning back in her seat.

They were quiet for a moment.

"So, do your teeth still feel weird?" Zoey asked.

Kate shrugged and turned to look out the bus window. "I'm getting used to it," she said.

Zoey knew Libby well enough already to know that her first reaction to being asked to model again would be the same as it was before: no.

Libby wasn't so much embarrassed by attention, like Kate was. She was just plain *shy*. And it didn't help that she was new to school or that she naturally stood out. She was five foot nine, covered with freckles, and wore her copper hair in a short bob. Libby was slowly but surely coming out of her shell, however, and had been such a good sport about the school fashion show that Zoey had hope she'd say yes again.

She waited to bring up the subject at lunch . . . and it started out pretty much as she'd feared.

"Couldn't I just take a picture of *you*?" asked Libby.

"I guess . . . ," Zoey said. "But I look so *young* . . . and you're so *tall* . . . you're more like a real model, you know?"

Libby pointed to Kate. "Kate's tall too. And, Kate, you could show off your new smile."

"She could," said Zoey, "but Kate *hates* having her picture taken. She always covers her face with her hands."

Kate stared at the ham-and-cheese sandwich she was working on and peeled off some crust. "In some parts of the world, you know, they think pictures steal your soul. . . ."

"But not in Mapleton!" Zoey laughed. "Come on, Kate. Tell Libby to do it."

Kate took the last bite of her sandwich. "You should do it," she said, crumpling her bag.

"Fine. Okay," Libby conceded, smiling. "Just tell me where and when, I guess."

"Yay! My house. This weekend," said Zoey. "We can do the fittings and the photo shoot then. Oh! Hey! But if you could maybe come over and go through my sketches with me, that would be great too. Want to come over today, even? Are you busy after school?"

"Yeah, totally," said Libby. "Now *that* part sounds like fun."

"How about you, Kate?" said Zoey. "Want to come over too?"

Kate, however, had already pushed her chair back and was gathering her trash. "Soccer game. Remember? We're playing the Cavendish School."

"Oh right. Well, how about this weekend?" said Zoey.

But Kate was already up and well on her way to the trash can.

CHAPTER 7

Vote for Your Favorite!

Okay. I did some serious fashion editing with my friend Libby last night, and we've narrowed my Avalon contest entry down to the two designs you see above. To say that it was HARD might be the understatement of the year. There are so many dresses I dream of making! Picking one is like having to choose one ride at an amusement park, you know?

But ultimately there were three criteria we knew the dress we picked had to meet (and if you're impressed with the word "criteria," you can thank my vocab word list this week.):

1) It had to be unique and cute! (Duh! Of course!)
2) It had to be right for one of the GORGEOUS fabrics I found at A Stitch in Time: a pink taffeta, an amazing off-white raw silk, and a cream brocade.
3) It had be something I could figure out how to make my own pattern for!

And so now, my dear Sew Zoey readers, it's YOUR turn to vote. And fast, if you don't mind! As you know, the contest deadline is THIS Sunday at midnight! So what do you think?

Should I go with A, the "Avalon" dress? Thanks to the wonders of Internet search engines, I discovered that Avalon was an island in Arthurian legend. I love anything medieval. (Just ask Mr. Dunn, my social studies teacher. I totally aced the Middle Ages unit.)

Or should I go with B, the pink "birthday cake" dress. This is my friend's favorite, since she loves pink more than life itself. White silk could be "the icing on the cake." Get it? ☺

So that's it! Cast your votes, ladies and gentlemen! Really. Vote now. Right this second. As soon as you can. As they say in Monopoly: "Do not pass GO. Do not collect two hundred dollars." Why? Because the sooner you vote, the sooner I can get started sewing. And because I can't wait to hear what you think!

By the time she posted her blog on Friday morning, Zoey was feeling good about her contest design. But no matter how hard she tried to ignore it, she was feeling weird about something else. Things just weren't right between her and Kate, and it was starting to feel heavy . . . like a wool coat that was really wet.

Zoey realized, when she thought about it, that she'd had the feeling on Thursday, too. But it wasn't until Kate climbed on the bus on Friday—and sat by herself right away in the front—that Zoey knew for sure something was really, truly wrong.

This was new for them. Zoey and Kate had been friends—best friends—since they were little, long before they started school. In all those years, they'd had just one fight Zoey could remember, which had lasted approximately one day—until Kate's mother suggested one take the hook and one take the eye patch, and they *both* could be lady pirates for Halloween back in first grade. Zoey knew everything about Kate, and Kate knew everything about her. At least, that's how it always had been. But it was different now. . . .

Of course, maybe Kate just needed space, Zoey thought. Maybe she needed to be alone. So Zoey sat back and tried to give it to her as the bus drove along. But when they got off, she couldn't stand it. Zoey hurried and followed her to the front door.

They both waved to Ms. Austen, who greeted them with a warm smile. She was wearing her Friday staple, a basic black dress, tall suede boots, and a soft ocher scarf.

"Good morning, Kate, Zoey," she told them. "Oh, Zoey," she added. "Stop by the office when you have a minute. A package came to your attention late yesterday afternoon."

"For me?" said Zoey.

"For you," Ms. Austen replied. "And it looks like it might be from the same Fashionsista who sent you the dress for the fashion show."

Zoey's jaw dropped a good half inch as a spark shot up her spine. Fashionsista was one of her earliest and most encouraging blog followers, whom Zoey had come to depend on for the most helpful fashion advice—and who had gone way above and beyond the call of duty when Zoey had her fashion disaster right before the school's fund-raiser fashion show. But why was she sending Zoey something now? Zoey wondered. She couldn't imagine what it could be. But if it was, indeed, from her fashion fairy godmother, Zoey couldn't wait to see!

"Thanks! Come with me!" she said, reaching for Kate . . . and coming away with an empty hand.

She looked around until she spotted Kate making her way toward a group of kids. They were waving her over to the trophy case, and one of them, Lorenzo, was pointing to a plaque. Zoey watched as

Kate joined them, and Lorenzo warmly patted her back.

Quickly, Zoey spun on her heels, glad the office was the other way.

That wet overcoat feeling? Suddenly it was twice as heavy.

It took Mrs. Beckstein, the secretary, a moment—and a few "ah-hem"s and "excuse me"s—to notice Zoey had walked in.

"Oh, hello there! Good morning," she said, looking up from her desk at last. "What can I do for you, dear?"

She pushed herself up and padded over to the counter, wearing a sweet, eager smile. Her hair was a bluer shade today, Zoey noticed. More hydrangea than lilac.

"Good morning. Ms. Austen said there was a package here waiting for me. . . ."

"Oh really? Okeydokey. Well, then, let's find it. What's your name again?" Mrs. Beckstein asked, setting her glasses on her nose.

"Zoey. Zoey Webber."

"Zoey Webber . . . ," the secretary repeated slowly as she shuffled to a mail cart near the wall. "Zoey Webber . . . no . . . no . . . no . . . Zoey Webber . . . Nope, not it . . ." She looked back. "Zoey Webber, did you say?"

"Yes, ma'am."

"Aha! Got it," Mrs. Beckstein said.

She picked up a small box—half the size of a box of tissues—and returned to Zoey and set it down.

Zoey read the label. Her name was printed clearly, followed by C/O MAPLETON PREP. And, sure enough, there in the upper-left corner was "Fashionsista."

"Something good?" asked the secretary, seeing Zoey's face light up.

"I don't know. I mean, I'm sure it is. But I don't know what . . ."

"Well, why don't you open it?" asked Mrs. Beckstein.

"Right," Zoey said. "Good idea!"

She carefully tore away the brown paper from the box, revealing a removable lid. Mrs. Beckstein was leaning over the counter, as eager as Zoey to see what it held. Zoey couldn't help noticing she smelled like the office—like coffee, paper, and hairspray.

"Well, lookit there," exclaimed the secretary as Zoey lifted the lid from the box. "Aren't those the cutest . . . What on Earth are they for, do you think?"

"Oh my gosh! They're labels!" Zoey said, and she knew *exactly* what they were for!

Fashionsista had sewn one just like them in the dress she'd remade for the fashion show. And now here were at least a hundred more, all saying the same thing—"Sew Zoey"—in the same exact font and color Zoey used in her blog!

And there was a note, Zoey suddenly noticed, tucked into one side. She pulled it out.

Dear Sew Zoey,
   Every Sew Zoey original should have a label, don't you think?
   Good luck with the contest— and keep up the good work!
   Fashionsista

"Aren't they amazing?!" Zoey beamed at Mrs. Beckstein from across the counter. "I can sew them into all my clothes!"

The secretary nodded, though she looked a bit doubtful. "Well, it'll keep you from losing them, I suppose. . . ."

Zoey dashed out of the office and toward her locker with the box tucked tightly under her arm. She wanted to make sure it was safely put away before first period, but at the same time she was dying to show them to someone.

Zoey passed by the trophy case. By then Kate and the others had gone. She glanced through the glass and noticed a clipping: "Mapleton Girls' Soccer Leads Conference; Kate Mackey Scores Tenth Season Goal." So that's what Lorenzo and everyone had been looking at. Kate must have had a really great game the day before. Zoey sighed, sorry she'd missed it. She wished Kate were there with her, so she could congratulate her right then. Well, she'd tell her later, Zoey decided . . . if Kate wasn't too busy with her *new* group of friends.

"Hey, Zoey!"

Zoey turned to see Libby, who'd just walked into school.

"What are you looking at?" Libby asked. "Oh wow! Good for Kate!" she said as she read the sports news.

"I know," said Zoey, nodding.

"So what's in the little box?"

"Oh yeah!" Zoey stood up a little straighter. "Check it out. These came to me at school!" She held up the box and opened it. "Fashionsista sent them. They're labels for my clothes!"

Libby gasped. "That's so cool! Do you know who Fashionsista is?"

Zoey shook her head. "I have no idea! I wish I did, though!"

"Well, she sure has perfect timing," said Libby. "You can put one in your contest dress."

"You're so right! I can!" Zoey smiled. The whole label idea was still sinking in. "And you're still coming over this weekend to take pictures, right?"

"Definitely," said Libby. "Have you decided which dress you're going to do?"

"Not quite . . . I actually put the final two sketches up on my blog for a vote."

"Good idea," said Libby, grinning. "Then I can vote for the pink one as soon as I get home!"

Zoey laughed, knowing how hard Libby had lobbied for the "birthday cake dress." The other dress was Zoey's favorite, but only by a tiny bit.

"By the way"—Zoey paused, gazing down—"I *love* those ombré jeans!"

They were skinny and white at the top, but somewhere just above knees they began to turn the faintest pink, which kept getting darker until they reached Libby's ankles, where they were full-on bubble gum.

"Thanks," said Libby. "I got them—"

"Don't tell me," Zoey said. "From your aunt."

"Yep." Libby nodded and twisted a springy red curl on her finger. "What can I say? She knows I like pink. I think she liked them mostly, though, because she's super into this whole ombré thing."

"Lucky! When can I meet her?" asked Zoey.

Libby shrugged. "I don't know," she mumbled. "We'll see."

Zoey dropped the subject. It was clear that was all Libby had to say, even though *why* she didn't want to talk about her aunt more, Zoey had no idea.

"I better go. Social studies," she told Libby. She checked the clock. "I'll be late if I don't run. Have fun in first period!"

"I'd tell you that too," said Libby. Her smile was back. "But I know you won't."

CHAPTER 8

The Results Are in: Ombré Everything!

Okay! This is the moment at least 243 of you (!) have been waiting for. The votes are officially in! And we have a winner, Sew Zoey fans: By a vote of 130 to 113, it's the "Avalon dress," the one inspired by the Middle Ages! Honestly, I can't thank all of you who voted enough for your help! Now I just have to make the thing . . . in forty-eight hours! . . . which is why I can practically guarantee you that I won't be blogging again until this dress is done! I really appreciate, by the way, all the suggestions that came for me to start the whole thing by making a muslin test dress. Who knew? And for the step-by-step directions, DressDiva, BIG thanks to you! I have the muslin fabric, and it's all ready to go. I just hope poor Marie Antoinette is prepared to be a pin cushion. . . . (Ouch! That's the life of a dress form, I guess.)

There's just one thing that might change, I'll warn you—which you can probably guess from the sketch above. I've discovered ombré! Yep! (It's pronounced om-bray and it means "to shade" in French.) Basically, they dip the fabric in dye, so the color changes gradually from dark to light. I'm in love. My friend Libby wore these fabulous ombré jeans to school today, and the idea's been stuck in my brain ever since. Thanks for the inspiration, Libby! So, I'm thinking I might take the off-white silk for the Avalon dress and ombré-cize it! Is that even a word? I don't know, but I'm going to try it.

Oh! And how could I forget?! I have one more

ginormous thank-you to shout out. This one goes straight to Fashionsista, who just sent me the best designer gift in the world: a whole box of Sew Zoey clothing labels! Real labels. Like, embroidered and professional-looking. Dear Fashionsista, if you're reading this, what would I ever do without you?!

At last. Zoey had the muslin test dress looking the way she wanted it. It was perfect.

Or at least, *very* close to perfect!

As soon as she counted all the votes that had come in, the rest of her Saturday was a blur. First, she had to make sure she had the dress sketched from every angle.

Then she pinned a big piece of plain, white muslin around the dress form, adjusting it so it fell in the right places on Marie Antoinette. Next, she cut out the shape of the neckline, pinned more fabric to the shoulders for the sleeves, and added the pieces of the skirt.

When the muslin looked right on the dress form, Zoey unpinned it and trimmed the pieces, allowing an extra inch for all the seams. She then used wide, loose basting stitches to temporarily hold the pieces together and put the basted dress back on Marie. When *that* part fit just right, Zoey slipped the muslin dress off the dress form and cut along the basted seams.

The pieces she was left with made a pattern— like the paper patterns she'd used before. And so from that point on, it was easy: pin it onto the Avalon fabric, cut out the pieces, and sew!

Uh-oh! she thought as she realized she cut one panel for the bodice a little too small. She tried to make it work, but the seam allowance began to fray, making the piece of fabric even smaller. In the end she had to recut the panel at the right size and try again.

Finally, she slipped the actual, mostly finished dress on Marie Antoinette.

Zoey stood back and rubbed her eyes. She was tired from a long day's work, but proud. Still, the longer she looked at the dress, the more she thought, *It sure is white. . . .*

She suddenly realized what she had was

basically a dress for a flower girl. Then she remembered Libby's ombré pants. Ombré was just what it needed.

Luckily, she had all kinds of dye left over from tie-dyeing the summer before. After she mixed up some violet dye, she dipped a swatch of fabric halfway in. Then she pulled it out of the dye, and kept dipping and pulling, letting less fabric go in each time. It was a little like the candle making she did with her class on their field trip to the pioneer town. And by the time she got to the edge, the fabric looked perfectly shaded, from white to purple—like a crocus when it bloomed.

The skirt and the sleeves of the actual dress took a bit longer, but they worked just as well, to Zoey's delight. It was way too late when she finally made her way to bed. And by the time she brushed her teeth and stumbled down the stairs Sunday morning, it was after ten a.m.

"Finally!" Her brother's shaggy head leaned out of the kitchen doorway. "We're *hungry!*" He let out a zombie moan. "I was about to make Dad go and wake you up."

"*Ugh . . .*" Zoey hung her head back. "I forgot it was Sunday. Do I *have* to make pancakes today?"

Sunday secret-ingredient pancakes had been a tradition in Zoey's family for years, and the tradition was basically this: Zoey and her dad made the batter and spiced it up with something different every week, while Marcus had to guess what was in them. If he failed, he had to do the breakfast dishes all by himself. He was usually pretty good at guessing—and Zoey was usually pretty kind. She'd toss in something superbasic like chocolate chips or bananas if she was feeling particularly nice. Last week, though, she tried to be tricky and added orange zest, fresh mint, and pomegranate seeds. The joke had ended up on Zoey, however, when Marcus guessed right, and the woody seed middles got stuck in *her* teeth.

Zoey looked over at Marie Antoinette, whose left sleeve was slipping down. She still had *so* much to do on her dress, she thought as she let out a weary yawn. "Do *you* want to make them today?" she asked, rubbing her eyes.

"And you guess what's in them?"

"Uh-huh." Zoey nodded. "Sure."

Marcus's face broke into a wide, sneaky grin. "Okay!" he said. "Done!"

A half an hour later breakfast was ready and Marie Antoinette's sleeve was firmly in place.

"Come and get it!" Zoey's dad called from the kitchen. "How's it going?" he asked as she walked in and took a seat.

"Good," Zoey said. "I still have a lot to do before Libby comes over, but it's getting there." She sniffed. The air was thick with . . . something. "Smells . . . *interesting*," she said.

She sat down as Marcus approached from the stove with a steaming platter piled high with pancakes the size of pizzas—the personal kind, at least.

"Ta-da!" he said, setting them down.

"Those are huge!" Zoey said.

"The bigger, the better," Marcus replied.

Zoey tried to study them for clues to what might be inside. But there was nothing very obvious . . . nothing more helpful than the warm, cakey smell. Zoey would have to rely on her sense of taste alone, it seemed.

"Well," Marcus said. "Dig in."

Zoey skipped the butter and syrup and cut off a piece with her fork and knife. She opened her mouth and popped it in and chewed as Marcus watched.

Hmm . . .

If there was a spice, she couldn't taste it. No, wait. Maybe she could. And only one thing could be so delicate. . . .

"Saffron. Right?" she guessed.

That's why the pancakes were so golden. It totally made sense.

Marcus looked at their dad. "Man, she's good. That was *his* idea, Zo, by the way."

"Nice try, Dad." Zoey smiled at him.

"I knew you'd get it," he said.

"And? What else?" said Marcus.

Zoey sighed and filled her fork again. *What else . . . ?* She took another bite.

"They're kind of crunchy . . . but I think I taste pineapple." She glanced at her dad. "Juice?"

He nodded proudly. "Bingo. Made it myself."

"Two down," Marcus said. "One secret ingredient left."

Another bite went in and Zoey slowly chewed. "I don't know. This is hard. . . . I think you put in too much salt."

"No excuses," Marcus said, chuckling. "So? Do you give up?"

"No," Zoey said stubbornly. "Wait . . . I know!"

There was another sense she could use, she realized. Feel. *What is that crunch?*

She took another bite to confirm the texture.

"Cornflakes!" she told Marcus.

"Nope." He shook his head.

"Rice Krispies?"

"Nope again."

"No?" Zoey sighed. "Oh fine. I give up."

"*Aw!* You were so close," said Marcus.

"So what is it?!" she asked as her dad laughed.

Marcus pumped his fist in victory. "I win! Potato chips!"

Marcus very sweetly offered to do the breakfast dishes for Zoey—*this* time—so she could get back to her dress. But a deal was a deal, Zoey told him, and besides, there wasn't *that* big a mess.

She returned to her dress as soon as she was finished. The ombré looked even better in the daylight. She still had to do the hem, but she had to wait for Libby to try on the dress. Oh, and her new labels. She couldn't forget to add one of those!

Zoey finished adding the label just as Libby arrived, and she ran to the door the second the bell rang.

"You're here!" she cried. "It's almost done!"

"Yeah?!" said Libby. "I can't wait to see it!" Then she paused. "Uh . . . what is that *sound*?"

"Oh, that?" Zoey shrugged off the clanging and banging that was blasting from the garage. She was so used to it, she realized, she hardly noticed it anymore. "It's just my brother," she told Libby. "Practicing drums. We have plenty of earplugs, by the way, if you want. Just let me know. Come on!"

She took Libby's hand and led her away from the noise and into the relatively peaceful dining room. "Ta-da!" She held her arms out toward Marie Antoinette. "I still need to hem it, but it's just about there. What do you think?"

"Oh my gosh! You dyed it! It's amazing!" Libby

clapped her hands and knit her fingers, holding them close up under her chin. "I love it! It's just like your sketch, only better! But . . ."

"But what?" Zoey said.

She turned back to the dress, searching for major flaws she'd overlooked.

"It's just that it looks like you don't need me, after all. You have a model already," Libby said.

She nodded to the fuzzy black gorilla mask, and Zoey had to laugh.

"Ah, yes." She went up and patted its head. "But she's camera shy."

Still giggling, Zoey lifted the furry rubber mask off the dress form and pulled it down over her own face.

"So," she went on, arms crossed. "The dress. You really like it? Be honest. I mean, could you see it in a store?" She tilted her head back so she could see through the eye slits.

Libby was nodding and laughing at her.

"I know you liked the birthday cake one better."

"I know," Libby said, "but that's just me. This is just as pretty."

"Why, thank you." Zoey bowed and tugged the gorilla mask off and used it to fan her hot, human face. "Enough monkey business." She smiled at Libby. "Are you ready to try it on?"

"Are you kidding? So ready!" said Libby.

"Well, what are we waiting for?" Zoey said. "Come on!" Gently, she lifted the dress off Marie Antoinette's shoulders and placed it in Libby's hands. "Let's go up to my room. You can change there, and then I can finish up the hem."

As she waited for Libby to put on the dress, Zoey didn't even realize she was holding her breath. It wasn't until Libby opened Zoey's bedroom door that she gulped for air at last.

"How do I look?" Libby asked. She smoothed the dress's front, just above the waist. Then she twisted her hips gently, swirling the flared skirt back and forth.

"Perfect!" Zoey said, holding out her arms. "How does it feel?"

"Really nice!" Libby said. "In fact, I wish you didn't have to hem it. I love it at exactly this length."

"You do?"

Zoey stood back and crossed her arms and eyed the bottom of the dress. It fell just below Libby's knees, which was far longer than Zoey had planned. But now that she saw in *on* Libby, she kind of liked how it looked as well. It had such a nice flow, and she knew when she hemmed it, that would change a lot. But the fabric frayed really easily, and Zoey couldn't leave the edge all raw like that . . . or could she?

She knelt down and gently began to pull at the loose strings dangling from the skirt.

"What are you doing?" Libby asked her.

"I'm not exactly sure. . . . But don't worry," Zoey said. "If it doesn't work, I'll just do the hem above the knee, the way I planned before."

She kept pulling and trimming when she needed to, until there was more than an inch of soft, frayed edge. It looked a little like she'd added fringe and a little like the fabric gradually disappeared. The effect, along with the ombré, was pretty cool.

She stood up and turned Libby's shoulders, so she could see herself in the mirror again. "What do you think?" Zoey asked.

"How'd you do that? It looks great!" said Libby. "You're totally going to win!"

"I hope so!" Zoey said. "Ready to take pictures?"

"Sure. That's what I'm here for. Let's go!"

Zoey had gotten her dad's good camera, the one with the big telescopic lens.

"So where do you want to take it?" asked Libby, turning to the mirror to check her hair.

"Hmm . . . I don't know," Zoey said.

She gazed around her cluttered bedroom. Somewhere under the collage of sketches and posters were her once-pink walls. And beneath the stacks of glossy magazines there was a desk, she thought. Zoey adored her room and wouldn't have had it any other way. But it was not exactly the best backdrop for a contest-winning fashion shoot.

"Outside?" Libby said, and Zoey nodded.

"Excellent idea!" Zoey crossed the room to her window and peered out at the backyard. "We could do it by my old playhouse. Or back against the fence."

They met Zoey's dad in the foyer. He was just putting on his coat. "Oh, hey, guys. Is that the contest dress? Libby, it looks wonderful on you!"

"Thanks." Libby smiled at Zoey.

"So where are you guys going now?"

"Outside," Zoey told him. "To take pictures. How about you?" She pointed to The Tie around his neck. "To work? I hope so."

He straightened it, grinning. "As a matter of fact, yes. There's a reception on campus. But I won't be gone long. I'll make dinner for you guys when I get back. Spaghetti sound good?"

They nodded, and he planted a kiss on Zoey's forehead, then waved a quick good-bye.

"Does everyone your dad works with have to wear ties like that?" Libby asked.

Zoey shook her head. "Oh no." She sighed. "No one but my dad . . ."

---------- CHAPTER 9 ----------

Ta-Da!

Hello! I'm back at the computer after a whirlwind weekend at the sewing machine. It's funny, though. . . . My dad always says, "It doesn't seem like work if you really love something," and I think I finally get what he means.

Anyhoo, my big news for today is that the contest dress is FINISHED, the pictures have been taken, and I am now officially entered in Avalon Fabrics' Break-Out Designer contest! I couldn't have done it without you all, either. Thanks for all your advice and tips! The muslin test dress worked perfectly. (I only wish I hadn't had to rip it apart. ☹) And much thanks to Dreamstress for the "start-with-a-new-needle" tip. I so wish I'd known about that before! It was like sewing butter this time. (Not that you'd ever want to do that, of course.)

Now, for those of you eagle-eyes who are thinking that the sketch above is a little different from my last sketch—you are right! I'll give you a minute to spot the differences. . . .

Okay! Time's up, ready or not!

Who said ombré? And who said the pockets are gone? Well, when I tried that ombré technique on the bottom part of the dress, those crown-shape pockets just felt like a little too much.

And who asked, "Sew Zoey, what happened to the hem?"

Good catch! And the answer? Well, in a nutshell, I decided to get rid of it. You see, my wonderful muse

on pins and needles

and model, Libby, liked the longer length, and honestly
so did I—but there wasn't enough fabric to keep it that
long and finish the bottom, too. But then I remembered
these napkins I made with my aunt Lulu and my friend
Kate when I was in third grade! We took squares of
some leftover fabric Aunt Lulu had, and she sewed a
line about a half an inch in from the edge all the way
around, then we pulled out all the loose threads running
all around all four sides, and it made the nicest fringe—
and I basically did the same thing here. Now I just hope
the contest judges love it as much as my great aunt
loved those napkins we gave her.

So now my contest entry is in and I guess all there
is to do is wait. Oh, and do a set of math problems and
answer four questions for social studies about ancient
Greece. And then, if I have time, start another quick
project. I'd tell you about it, but it's a surprise!

Oops.

Zoey closed her blog and checked the time. Eight
o'clock. If she started now, she could whip out a
new and much improved ESU tie for her dad, no
prob. She only wished she'd thought of it a week

ago. After all, she had plenty of purple and gold fabric left, and ties looked easy to make. Zoey was sure she could finish it, along with her homework, before it got too late.

She started to close her laptop, but decided to check her e-mail first.

Oh wow!

There in her in-box was another message from Cecily@CChen!

Dear Zoey,

I'm so happy to hear that you're entering the Avalon contest—and I wish you the very best of luck! I've really enjoyed reading about your process and seeing your sketches on your blog. I was also wondering if you remember that mass-market line I was telling you about? The one I'm doing for tweens? Well, it's done too, I'm excited to say, and so I know exactly how you feel. And since you are the only tween I know—and a style guru to boot—I thought, who better to share it with? Any chance you could take a look and let me know, in your expert opinion, what you think of it?

A million thanks!
Your friend in fashion,
   Cecily

Zoey eagerly opened the attachment to see a whole series of sketches, all drawn by Cecily Chen herself. There was everything! Jeans, jackets, sweaters, party dresses, and casual skirts—all with a distinctive, classic Cecily Chen look. Zoey felt as if she were in some kind of incredible fashion dream, and as she flipped through the sketches, she had to keep reminding herself to relax and breathe.

Zoey couldn't wait to write back to the designer as soon as she was done.

Dear Cecily,
Thank you so much for sharing your sketches with me! Honestly, I love them all! The sherbet colors are gorgeous and such a great change from last season's jewel tones. And the boatneck tops! I would totally buy them, and so, I think, would all my friends, who all have VERY different tastes. Really, you seem to have something for every kind of style, which is so

cool!, from glitter to denim to that flutter-sleeved shirt that I just know my friend who LOVES anything pink and frilly would ADORE! There's only one thing I'm not totally crazy about . . . and that's the cargo pants. I can't believe I'm actually saying this—and feel free to ignore it totally, please!—but would they look better without all the pockets, by any chance, do you think?

Thank you, thank you, thank you again! And feel free to send me any designs anytime! Please!
Your friend in fashion forever!

Zoey
PS Oh! And have I said that I loved, loved, loved your book? Loved it.

Monday was such a big day, but it didn't start quite the way Zoey had hoped. She would've loved to have met Kate on the bus and to tell her all about Cecily Chen's e-mail and about finishing the dress. And she would have loved to have heard how Kate's weekend went and about everything she had done. Zoey had never gone so many days without talking to Kate, and she realized she missed her. A lot. But then Kate climbed on the bus and they looked at each other . . . and neither one said a word.

Kate sat down, alone, in the front again, and that's how they rode to school.

Zoey slid to the edge of her seat. Should she talk to Kate? But what could she say? She couldn't decide, and before long, the bus pulled into the school parking lot and Zoey hadn't said anything. It was too late.

At lunch later that day, Priti was back from visiting her family in Canada. She sat down with Zoey at their usual table, eager to hear *everything*. Zoey almost forgot that Kate wasn't talking to her, since Priti talked enough for both of them.

"So what did I miss?" Priti asked as she took a bite. "I read your blog, of course, but that's just the beginning. Right?"

Zoey told her how hard she and Libby had worked and about the Sew Zoey labels she'd received from Fashionsista. "And guess what? I got another e-mail from Cecily Chen last night!" she said as Priti's eyes followed Kate, who had her lunch tray but was walking past their table.

"Kate!" Priti waved over Zoey's head. "Where are you going? Get over here!"

Zoey sighed. She was just about to tell Priti that Kate had started to sit with the girls on her soccer team when she saw Kate smile at Priti and change her course toward them.

Kate took the other seat next to Priti. "How was your grandparents' anniversary?" she asked.

"*So* many relatives," Priti told them. "But it was really, really nice. And I got to wear an *amazing* sari!"

"Ooh! Do you have pictures?" Zoey asked.

"Tons!" Priti said. "My phone's in my locker, but I'll show you after school. Wait! You were saying you got another e-mail from Cecily Chen last night. What did it say? Oh, hang on! There's Libby. Hi!" she yelled, cupping her hand around her mouth.

Libby weaved her way over through the maze of tables and slid in on Zoey's other side. "Hey, Priti! Welcome back!"

"So! I hear you've been doing more modeling!" said Priti.

Libby blushed and tugged on her bangs. "I don't know if I'd call it *that*. But it was pretty fun. Oh, but guess what I just found out?" She suddenly turned to face Zoey with eyes that said *Big news!*

"What?" Zoey asked. She tried, but she couldn't tell at all if the big news was good . . . or bad.

"Last night my mom called my aunt and they were talking, and guess what she said."

"What? *What?*" Zoey asked again as Libby drew in a deep breath.

"My aunt's one of the judges for the Avalon contest!"

"Your *aunt*? Really? No way!" said Zoey. She grinned . . . then frowned. Was that good or bad?

"I couldn't believe it either," said Libby. "I had no idea."

"Me either . . ." Zoey glanced across the table at Kate, who was looking at her kind of weird.

"But then you know what?" Libby went on. "I looked at the website, and her name was right there."

"But that's great! Don't you think?" said Priti. "Zoey has to win now, right?!"

Libby frowned and so did Zoey. Kate was suck-
ing her lip.

"No, of course not," Zoey said as she turned to
Libby. "But it's . . . okay, isn't it?" she asked. She'd
already sent the picture in, and she didn't know
what she would do if it turned out that she broke
some rule. . . .

Libby nodded slowly. "Yeah. It's okay. I couldn't
enter the contest, but if I'm just in a picture, it's no
big deal."

"Phew!" Zoey let out a breath, heavy with relief.
"You had me worried for a second."

"Sorry," said Libby.

It was a little strange for Zoey to come home from
school on Monday and not have a huge project waiting for her. There was no reason to rush through
her homework or leave her English reading for
some other day. Zoey finished her math and did
her Spanish and even answered extra-credit questions for good old Mr. Dunn. Then she checked and
double-checked the Avalon Fabrics website to make
sure her contest entry was received and that there

was truly no rule against judges' relatives modeling clothes. . . .

After that, while she waited for her dad to get home from work, she finally had time to think about her day. Overall, it had been fine. But in one *huge* way it had been awful—and it had to do with Kate.

She'd gotten hopeful when Kate came over and sat at their table for lunch. But Kate still hardly said a word to Zoey, and then she got up and left before they were done. Zoey wondered if Kate wanted to hang out with the girls from her soccer team . . . and all those boys who liked her so much.

Zoey looked at the clock and realized Dad would be home soon. She put a thin gift box on the hall table so it would be there waiting for him. In the meantime she decided to start a new project. She flipped through her sketchbook and saw the pink dress Libby loved so much. She decided to make it as a thank-you for Libby for her help with the contest. After all, it was a very Libby kind of dress!

Zoey was busy working on the muslin pattern for the "Libby dress" when she heard her dad come home from work. She ran to greet him.

"What's this?" he asked as he put down his keys and picked up the package.

"Open it!" Zoey said.

He untied the satin ribbon and let the wrapping paper slip away.

"Zo, this is great!" he said right away. He held up the tie and turned to the mirror. "Sharp," he declared with a wink. Then he glanced back at her over his shoulder. "But I thought you weren't so crazy, Zo, about ESU ties?"

"I'm not crazy about your *old* one," Zoey told him. "Those eagles are *crazy*. Insane. Purple and gold are perfectly sane, I think—in moderation."

Her dad nodded. "I see. Well, I love it! You really made this?"

Zoey grinned and reached for the tie and turned it over. "See for yourself," she said.

On the back, she'd neatly sewn a Sew Zoey label.

"Nice!" he said with an approving nod. "Very professional. Where'd you get these from?"

"Oh, didn't I tell you?" she said. "A whole box-ful came to school last week. My blog follower,

Fashionsista, sent them! Remember? The one who saved the day at the fashion show."

Zoey was beaming . . . but her dad's smile was fading, faster and faster, until it went flat.

"What?" she asked as he rubbed his chin. "What's the problem?" she asked again.

He sighed. "I have to tell you, Zo, I wasn't so thrilled when that first package went to your school, but it really did save the day, and so . . . Well, I let it slide. But a second package? I don't know. It's just not good, I think, for strangers to find out so much about you from your blog."

Zoey couldn't help groaning. "But, *Dad*! This is from *Fashionsista*! She—"

Her dad held up a finger. "Or he," he said.

"Or *he*. But I really think she is a she. And I swear she is *fine*," Zoey told him.

"Yes, she probably is," her dad agreed. "But that's not the case for everyone out there in the world. And you can't be too careful on the Internet about protecting your privacy, that's for sure."

"Fine," Zoey said. "You're right. But it's not like I post my address or anything. I mean, don't you trust that I know better than that?"

"I know," said her dad, "but I think you could still be a lot more careful." He paused and seemed to think. "How 'bout this, Zo. Let me go into your blog, okay, and see what should be changed."

"What?" Zoey's lip curled up in horror. She whipped her head from side to side.

"I won't *rewrite* it," her dad assured her. "I just want to make sure there's nothing too personal, which is what I really should have been doing the whole time."

"But, Dad . . ." Zoey didn't mean to pout, but there was nothing else to do. "It's *supposed* to be personal. Don't you get that? It's my *blog*."

"I mean personal *information*," he explained. "Stuff that strangers shouldn't know. If you give me your admin info, I'll take a look at it all tonight."

Zoey's shoulders sank. Her lip slid out. She hugged her arms across her chest. She knew just how Cinderella felt at midnight when her shimmery ball gown turned to rags.

"Fine." She sighed. "But *please* don't change too much!" she begged.

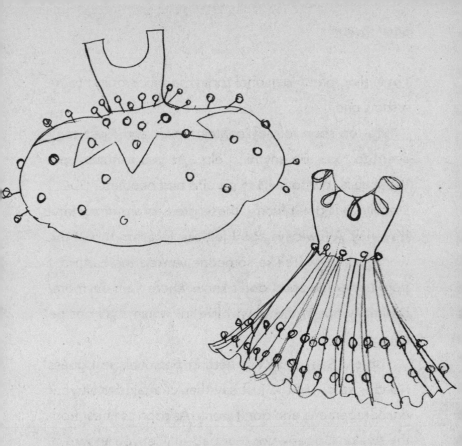

------- CHAPTER 10 -------

On Pins and Needles

Hola! (That's "hi!" in case you don't take Spanish.) Sorry I haven't been blogging much for the last few days. It turns out my dad thought I was getting too personal or giving away too many details or something. I don't know how to write without getting personal, and

I'm feeling pretty personal today, so this is going to be a short one.

It's too soon for any contest news, and I just can't seem to focus on anything else. As you can see from the sketch I did today, I'm on pins and needles—LOL—literally! But don't worry, these dresses are imaginary! It's funny. A few days ago I felt like I was on top of the world, and now it's like someone yanked the Earth out from under me and I don't know where I am anymore. Definitely not in the town I live in, which shall not be named.

Uh-oh! See? Now I'm getting personal, so I guess I better stop. Let me just say thanks again for all your encouragement, and don't worry. As soon as I hear from the Avalon judges—good or bad—I'll let you know.

"Ouch!" Zoey jumped at the pinch on her arm and, wincing, spun around. "What'd you do that for?" she asked Priti, who was standing behind her in the school hallway and clearly enjoying herself.

"Thought you'd be used to it," said Priti. "Since you're a human pincushion and all."

"Very funny," said Zoey. She rubbed her arm. With her foot, she closed her locker door. She grinned. "I guess you read my blog."

"Of course," said Priti. "Wouldn't miss it. But what's the no personal stuff about? I don't get it."

Zoey shook her head. "My dad." She groaned. "He wants to make sure strangers don't know too much about me, so can you believe it"—Zoey still couldn't—"he's *censoring* me now."

Priti's eyes got big. "What?" she asked.

"Yeah," Zoey replied. She glanced down to make sure she had the right notebooks before she clicked her lock. "He has my admin info and he's—" She began to go on, just as Priti called, "Hey, Kate!" across the emptying hall.

Zoey looked up. Her eyes met Kate's, but just for a second, as she walked up.

"Hi . . . Priti," Kate said, flashing their friend a tight smile, hiding all but a line of her movie-star teeth. She started to pause, or at least Zoey thought she did. But then she seemed to think again. "See you later," she said, very plainly to Priti. "Better hurry or I'll be late to gym."

Zoey, along with Priti, watched Kate walk away. Zoey knew Priti had to be thinking, the same thing.

"What's up with you two?" Priti asked her.

Zoey shrugged. "I wish I knew."

"Did something happen?" asked Priti. There was a half-panicked look on her face. "Did you guys have a fight or something while I was away?"

Zoey wanted to laugh. "I *wish*," she said honestly. "Then I could say sorry and we could make up. But it's not me. It's Kate. It's like she's a different person since her braces came off, you know?"

"Different? What do you mean?" said Priti. "She seems the same to me."

"Well, you haven't been around," Zoey told her. "But just wait. You'll start to see. It's like all of a sudden she's hanging out with different people. *Boys* especially."

"Ah . . ." Priti arched a fine, dark eyebrow. "Boys like Lorenzo, do you mean?"

"No." Zoey frowned.

Priti smiled a half smile and hugged her books tighter.

"Well . . ." Zoey reconsidered. "Okay, maybe."

"Okay." Priti nodded. "But I still don't really know what you're talking about. Kate's always hung out with boys, Zo, you know that. At least the ones who play sports." She put her hand on Zoey's shoulder. "If it's not a fight you guys had, then it's got to be something else. I think you guys should talk, Zo, and sort the whole thing out."

Zoey sighed and turned and closed her lock so gently that she had to do it again. *Is Priti right?* she asked herself. *Will talking even help? Or is it too late?*

She offered a weak smile to Priti. "I guess I'll try," she said.

The question then of course was, when? And how? And what would she say?

Priti answered those questions for Zoey, however, by leading Kate to their table at lunch.

"Kate, Zoey wants to talk to you," Priti said simply. "Zoey, go ahead. I'm going to the salad bar, and I want everyone happy—and talking to each other!—by the time that I get back. Understand?"

They both watched Priti wave and walk off. Zoey watched Kate sigh and take a seat.

"So what do you want to talk about?" asked Kate.

"This wasn't my idea, but I want to talk about us, I guess," Zoey said, shrugging.

"Okay." Kate nodded . . . and waited. "What about us?" she asked. She put her elbow on the table and rested her chin on her hand. "I don't know why you care so much about us when you have Libby now. It's like you don't even need me anymore."

"Huh?" Zoey said, confused. Had the world just totally turned inside out? She was hearing Kate say things to *her* that she wanted to say to Kate. "I don't know what you're talking about," said Zoey. "You're the one who is hanging out with new friends!"

Kate leaned forward across the table. "Well, you're the one who won't hang out with me anymore. Anyway, it's fine," Kate added, crossing her arms. "If you want to *delete* me from your life and make Libby your new best friend because she has designer clothes and a famous aunt, go ahead."

Zoey's mouth fell, along with her stomach, her heart, her lungs, and her brain. She wasn't sure what was worse at that very moment: Kate thinking she'd really do that or Libby walking up at that very moment and hearing the words come from Kate. The look on Libby's face was one she'd never seen before. It was a mash-up of hurt and mad and lost and sad, plus a little just-seen-a-ghost.

Zoey was still in shock when Libby dashed in the opposite direction, and Kate slid out of her chair and walked away.

Priti walked up a few minutes later with a plate of pasta salad, tomatoes, and bread.

"So what happened?" she asked, sitting down at the nearly empty table.

Zoey slumped over her unopened lunch bag. "You don't want to know." She moaned.

Zoey barely made it through the door of her house before the tears began to pour. She'd worked hard to keep them in at school, but she couldn't hold them anymore. Somehow, in one lunch period, she'd managed to lose two of her best friends. And to think that she'd been feeling as if her life were falling apart before. That was nothing compared to this, she realized. *This* was the end of the world.

She pulled the door closed behind her and turned . . . and nearly fell.

"Zo? Is that you?" she heard Marcus call. "There's a box for you in the hall!"

No kidding, she thought, looking straight down at the knee-high cardboard box.

That woman from the fabric store brought it.

"What is it?" he asked, walking in from the kitchen. "Whoa? What happened? What's wrong?"

"Nothing," she said, bending down, letting her hair fall over her face. She sniffed and read the label. "Oh my gosh!" She gasped. "It's from Cecily Chen!"

Marcus clapped his hands. "Wow! Awesome!" he said. "Who's that?"

"Who's *that*?" Zoey yanked at the top of the box to pry it open, but the flaps were firmly taped shut. "She's only a *real* fashion designer! I need some scissors!" she said, jumping up. She ran to the kitchen, but the scissors weren't in their usual spot.

"How about these?" she heard Marcus call out from the dining room, and she ran to see what he had found.

"No!" she cried as soon as she saw them: her

precious razor-sharp dressmaker shears. "Those are for fabric! I don't want them to get dull!"

"Okay." He set them back down next to the sewing machine. "Just trying to help . . . How about this?" he asked, holding up her tracing wheel.

Now, that might work, thought Zoey. The tracing wheel was like a pizza cutter, but tiny, with zillions of itsy-bitsy teeth. It was specifically for transferring marks from patterns onto fabric—with the help of tracing paper slipped in between.

"Let's try it," Zoey told him.

Back in the foyer, she ran the wheel over and over the box's taped seams until it broke through at last. She tugged and yanked till she pried the flaps open.

"Well? What's in it?" Marcus asked.

"No way!" Zoey exclaimed.

Inside were clothes. Sherbet-colored clothes. Pale greens and yellows and pinks . . . Zoey couldn't see what they all were, exactly. They were neatly folded and stacked. But then she realized that they looked familiar. She had already seen them—in Cecily Chen's e-mail!

There was an envelope on top of the pile, and Zoey plucked it out. Inside was a folded note. She had to pause to sniff and wipe her eyes as she read it through two times.

Dear Zoey,

You said you thought there was something in my new tween line for all your friends, so I thought I'd send you a few samples that you could share with all of them. It's the least I can do to thank you for reviewing them for me. You might notice, by the way, there aren't any cargo pants— and that's because you were so right; they look infinitely better without pockets, and the orders have doubled since I made the change. You clearly know your stuff!

Please enjoy—and tell your friends I hope they enjoy them too!

Your friend in fashion, as always,
Cecily

Just then the front door opened and Zoey's dad walked in.

"Hey there!" he said, staring down at the box. "What's all of this?"

Zoey sat back on her heels. "Don't worry, Dad. It's not from a stranger!" she said. "It's from Cecily Chen, the designer I met at A Stitch in Time."

"So . . . why do you look so upset?" he asked slowly. He glanced down the hall at Marcus.

"Don't look at me," Marcus said, and shrugged. "I was wondering the same thing."

"It's complicated," Zoey told them. She wiped her nose with the back of her hand. "But it's not because of this." She looked down at the note again, sadly, and read it once more to herself.

Please enjoy—and tell your friends . . .

Friends. What *friends?* was all she could think. As of that afternoon, Priti was her only friend. Libby had overheard what Kate said at the lunch table, then turned and marched away. Kate had fled as well without saying a word. Zoey couldn't have given these fabulous clothes to them now even if she tried. And why? Because of *nothing*—at least nothing that was true. Seriously! How could Kate say Zoey didn't need *her*, when *she* was the one hanging out with new friends? And didn't Kate and Libby both know her better than to think Zoey would use Libby and her aunt to win?

"Is there anything I can do?" asked her dad.

Zoey looked up and sighed. "Can you make my friends not hate me?"

"Hate you? What happened? Why?"

"I wish I knew," said Zoey.

"Well, that's the first step," her dad said.

"What do you mean?"

"You have to figure it out," her dad said, "and then take it from there."

"Right," Zoey said softly. She leaned back and hugged her shins. *Rrrippp*. Suddenly the denim across her knee split.

Great! She put her head down on her knee and rubbed the hole with her chin. What good were her favorite jeans now, she thought, when they looked like this?

And what good was a box full of amazing Cecily Chen clothes when she had no one to share them with?

---------- CHAPTER 11 ----------

Fabric Fixes

Patches! Don't you love them? I do! More than anything, as of today! Not only can they make a bold, colorful statement, like in these outfits here, but they're practical, too! What better way is there to save something you can't live without if it ever gets a hole?

sew zoey

Like my jeans, which just ripped today (which was about the last thing I needed right then). This was a simple case of being worn—and loved—way too much. (And probably of crawling around too much, hemming skirts on Marie Antoinette.) Sure, I could leave my jeans religious (a.k.a. "holy" LOL). But I've never really been a big fan of that distressed-denim look. And the hole will just get bigger and bigger, I know, until my whole knee starts poking out. I could also cut them off, I guess, and make them into shorts. But *both* my knees would show then, and when it gets cold I would freeze. No, the only answer to saving the best jeans in the whole world, I've decided, is to make a patch—to find a cute, durable piece of fabric; a needle; and some strong thread and to carefully sew it over that little hole before it gets too big. But first, I'm afraid, I have some other holes I also need to patch. . . .

(Hey, I think I just made up a metaphor there. My English teacher would be so proud!)

Zoey had two friendships to patch up, and she couldn't wait till the next day to start. She found her phone and picked it up . . . then put it down.

"Dad!" she called. "I'm going out."

He popped his head out of the kitchen as she ran down the stairs. "Where are you going? Dinner's almost ready."

"Just over to Kate's for a sec." She paused. "What are we having?" she asked.

"Stir fry," he told her. "And sesame noodles." He waved a springy, sauce-covered whisk.

"Yum!" Zoey said. Of her dad's dinner repertoire, this was definitely up there with the best. She blew a kiss as she grabbed her jacket and pulled open the front door. "I'll be back as soon as I can!" she told him. "If you want to eat, though, go ahead."

Kate's house was just two streets away, but it took forever, it seemed, to get there. Zoey started off walking, then walked faster, until she was half-running by the end. She got to the mailbox by the sidewalk that looked like a miniature version of Kate's yellow house. It had the same shingled roof and glossy white trim, and even a chimney jutting up near the back. Zoey turned and galloped up the neat brick walkway, between the rows of purple mums. She leaped up the stairs to the porch and rapped the shiny brass knocker and rang the doorbell at the same time.

A moment later, she heard footsteps, and the door opened wide.

"Zoey! Why, hello!" said Kate's mother. "What a lovely surprise." She wiped her hands on the frilly apron that shielded her corduroy skirt and tartan plaid blouse. "Is something wrong?" she asked with a warm but curious smile.

"No, I'm . . . good, Mrs. Mackey." Zoey automatically smiled back. "Um . . ." She peered around her shoulder. "Is, uh, Kate around?" she asked.

"Well . . ." Kate's mom paused, as if that was a tricky question. "You know, we were just about to sit down. . . ."

"Oh, I'm sorry." Zoey could suddenly smell something hot and meaty simmering inside. "But it's kind of important, and it won't take long. . . ."

"School stuff?" Mrs. Mackey asked.

Zoey nodded. Kind of.

"Well, then, come right in." Kate's mom stepped back to make room for Zoey to pass. "She's in her room. Go on up. And tell her that dinner's going to be on the table soon."

At the top of the stairs Zoey gently knocked on Kate's door, the one to the right. The door was open, and Zoey could see Kate stretched out across her bed. Her headphones were on, and her face was covered by the book they were reading in English class.

Kate didn't hear the knock at first, but after a second, her head turned. She sat up and pulled off her headphones while Zoey took a big gulp of air.

"Can I come in?"

"I guess . . . yeah, sure," Kate said. She scooted over. "Uh . . . want to sit down?"

Zoey nodded and took a seat at the foot of Kate's bed, on the green gingham bedspread that Kate had had for as long as Zoey could remember.

"I just wanted to say . . . I'm sorry," said Zoey.

"You are?" Kate's face, which had been stony, softened just a little bit.

Zoey nodded. "Uh-huh. But you're wrong. I *don't* want to delete you from my life at all—or not be your best friend." She tugged at the hole in the knee of her jeans, which still needed to be patched. "In fact, it seems like the other way around to me. It seems like . . . ever since you got your braces off . . . you've been avoiding *me* and hanging out with other kids instead."

"Avoiding *you*?" Kate threw her head back. "Oh my gosh. That's *so* not true."

"No?"

"No. I mean, what? Are you talking about the soccer team?"

Zoey shrugged and nodded again.

"Well, they're my teammates," Kate explained.

"Are the boys your teammates too?"

"*Boys?*" Kate made a creeped-out face. "Who wants to hang out with them?"

"Uh, *you*," Zoey informed her.

"I do not!" Kate declared. She crossed her arms and frowned at Zoey, then shook back her hair. "But if you're going to ditch me because I'm not fashiony enough, then I guess why shouldn't I hang out with them?"

"But I didn't ditch you," said Zoey.

Kate looked away and twisted her mouth. "You

deleted me, Zo." She sighed. "How much clearer could you be?"

Zoey threw her head back this time. "Why do you keep saying that? I don't even know what you *mean*."

"You deleted me from your blog. It was bad enough when you started to hang out with Libby instead of me, but then you actually went in and took my name out of old blog posts. I mean, I helped you start Sew Zoey, and now it's like I'm not even part of your life anymore."

"*Deleted* you from my blog?" Zoey frowned. That made no sense . . . at first. "My blog . . ." She repeated, slowly this time. "My *dad*, of course!"

"Zoey, what are you talking about?" Kate asked.

"I didn't delete you. My dad did," Zoey explained. "He went on this whole privacy kick the other day and went in and cut out people's names and all kinds of stuff. I'm so sorry. I didn't realize what it would look like to you."

"Privacy kick? But why would he cut out my name?" Kate stuck out her lip.

Zoey shrugged. "I think he thought he was

protecting you. But don't worry, we'll put you back in." She grinned. "And if my dad thinks first names are too personal, we can make up fake names. How about that? Hey!" She held up a finger . . . and so did Kate, at just the same time.

"Are you thinking what I'm thinking?" said Kate.

"Lorelei and Penelope?" they both said together. "Yes!" the two of them cried.

Those were the names they'd called themselves when they played "grown-up girls" in first grade. Zoey had been Penelope, an artist, archaeologist, and part-time flight attendant who could talk to most animals. Lorelei was Kate's play-name, and she was an Olympic soccer star who also baked cupcakes and was a deep-sea diving instructor.

Kate laughed, then she sighed. "Still," she said softly. "You have been kind of weird, Zo. Like whenever you see me, you turn away."

"I'm sorry," said Zoey. "I didn't mean to. I guess I was just trying to give you space . . . and . . ." There was the other reason—a bigger one, even—that she was suddenly embarrassed to say.

"What?"

"I was . . . jealous."

"You were jealous?" Kate's face scrunched up. "Of what? Of me?"

Zoey took a deep breath and tried her best to explain—to herself and Kate.

"It's dumb, I know. But I couldn't help it."

"But why? What did I do?" said Kate.

"You didn't do anything," Zoey told her, "except get your braces off, I guess . . . and then, remember how Lorenzo said you looked so awesome last week at lunch?"

Kate shook her head blankly. "No."

"Really?" said Zoey. "You don't?"

Kate shook her head again. "No, but that's just Lorenzo—he says 'awesome' all the time. . . ."

"*Now* you tell me." Zoey groaned. "I wish I'd known that the day before. I got all excited—like it was special—when he said it to me. And then the next day when he said it to you . . . It was like, no one's ever going to like me now when Kate's so pretty."

"Oh my gosh!" said Kate. She rolled back on her bed.

"I know. I said it was stupid." Zoey giggled. "But it kind of is true."

"No, it isn't at all. And most important, who cares? I mean . . . *Do* you like Lorenzo?" she asked, popping back up.

Zoey thought about it for a second. "I don't know. Maybe. A little. What about you?"

"Me? Uh-uh," Kate told her. "He's too short for me, anyway."

They both laughed. Then they hugged. Then Kate's mom called from below.

"Kate? Zoey? How are you girls coming up there? We're ready to eat down here. Zoey? Would you like to stay and have some pot roast, sweetie?"

Kate looked at Zoey hopefully, but Zoey shook her head.

"No, thanks, Mrs. Mackey!" she hollered back. "It smells really good, but I should go home and eat with Marcus and my dad." She turned back to Kate. "Just one more thing . . . ," she said.

"Yeah?"

"About Libby . . . and her aunt. I just hope you know . . . I mean, you must know . . . that I didn't, and I wouldn't, ask Libby to model because of her aunt. . . . And I had no idea until Libby told us that she was a contest judge, I swear."

Zoey couldn't imagine Kate not believing her, but she studied Kate's face just the same. Was there any doubt? She didn't think so. But it would be nice to know for sure. . . .

"Oh, I know, Zo. I didn't really think that. I was just so . . . hurt and mad." Kate bit her lip. "I should probably tell her that, huh?"

"Would you?" Zoey had to hug her again. "That would be so great! Thanks!" she said.

Zoey took a deep breath. It felt so good to patch things up with Kate. Maybe things were finally getting back to normal.

-------------- CHAPTER 12 ---------

Mending Friendships

Patches. I still love them. Will always love them. But I have to agree with some comments that came in. You do have to be careful not to go overboard. You really can end up looking like a hobo if you go too crazy with them. That's why I'd like to thank Fashionsista (again!)

for suggesting another excellent way to repair a hole: reweaving! Have you heard of it? I hadn't until now. It's where you take threads from the fabric itself and use it to fill the hole so that it basically disappears. It sounds a little tricky, but it's worth it. They say the fabric is just as strong, if not even stronger, in the end. It's good to know there are so many ways to fix things that tear, don't you think? All it takes is a little attention and patience . . . and maybe a needle and some thread.

Not to get too deep or dramatic, but all this talk of mending fabric is making me think of mending fences. I'm going through a friendship emergency! Turns out they're much harder than fashion emergencies. I'm doing everything I can think of to mend things before it's too big to fix. But I miss how it was when I was little. All you had to do was give a friendship bracelet to a friend and that was it: friends forever. Will it ever be that easy again?

I drew this dress based on how friendship bracelets are woven. But right now, it still feels like things are in danger of unraveling. I'm working on a peace offering to patch another friendship hole. I sure hope it works.

Oh, and as far as the contest goes, sorry, still nothing

to report—just an e-mail basically saying that they'd be in touch "soon." I wish I knew what "soon" meant. I'll let you know when I find out!

"Libby!"

Zoey and Kate ran up to Libby together as soon as they saw her get off her bus. She froze, and Zoey watched her face go through a million expressions in a row. Zoey hoped it would stop on something like "pleasantly surprised." But no. It kept on going until it settled on "gloomily annoyed."

"Hey!" Kate said as they reached her.

"Yeah?" Libby said stiffly.

Kate put a hand to each shoulder to balance her backpack and took a bracing breath. "I just want to say sorry about that stuff I said about Zoey liking you just for your aunt. It was totally dumb and not true at all. . . . I just said it because I was mad."

Libby listened, but her face didn't change much. "What did *you* have to be mad at?" she asked Kate.

"Well . . ." Kate switched her weight from foot to foot. "I was jealous, I guess."

"Of me?" Libby looked from Kate to Zoey.

Kate shrugged. "A little bit."

"We were jealous of each other," Zoey tried to explain. But making sure Libby knew they liked her for *her* was the most important thing. "Really, Libby, I liked you—*we* liked you—way before we knew about your aunt. I had no idea she was a judge when I asked you to model my dress."

"Well, how about when you made it ombré?" muttered Libby. Her eyes were hard and cold.

"No!" said Zoey. "Of course not! I just liked it . . . really . . . and I thought it would look good! Besides, you didn't even tell us your aunt was a judge until after the dress was done."

"It was right there on the website," said Libby. "You totally could have looked."

"Well, yeah, I could have, I guess," said Zoey. "Except that I still don't know her name. I went back and looked at the list on the website yesterday even, and I didn't know who she was."

This seemed to soften Libby a little. But she still looked sore and stung.

"I never told you her name?" she asked softly.

Zoey and Kate both shook their heads.

Kate spoke up. "Seriously, Libby, I've known Zoey almost my whole life, and she would never cheat or use a friend. I knew that when I said it . . . and I'm really sorry that I did."

Kids were rushing past them to get to homeroom before the bell rang. But Libby stood very still. She looked at Zoey and smiled, sighing. "I guess I'm sorry too," she said. "It's just . . . at my last school I had this friend—I thought she was my *best* friend, in fact—but really she just liked me because of my aunt. She actually said she'd stop being my friend if I ever stopped giving her the stuff my aunt sent me. . . ."

"So what'd you do?" asked Zoey.

"I gave it to her," Libby said. "Until my mom found out and made me stop . . ."

"Then what happened?"

"She stopped being my friend," said Libby, "just like she said. And then she told everyone else to stop talking to me. And they did."

"That's terrible!" said Zoey.

"That's awful!" Kate declared.

Libby sniffed and nodded. "All I can say is I was glad when we moved," she said.

"Well, we're glad too," said Zoey. "And we're not like that girl."

"We'd never do that!" said Kate. "What an unbelievable jerk!"

"We'll always be here for you," Zoey told Libby. Then she raised her arm. From her hand dangled a large, crinkly paper shopping bag. "Here. In fact, I want to give something to you."

"What is it?" Libby asked.

"I made it for you the other night. Before . . . everything," Zoey said. "It's a thank-you gift for all your help with the contest."

Libby took the bag and peeked inside. Zoey could hear her gasp. She started to smile, and as she did, Zoey started to smile as well.

"Oh my gosh," Libby said.

Inside was the pink, ruffled, "birthday cake dress" that Libby had loved so much as a sketch. It had actually turned out so well, she should have entered it in the contest, Zoey thought.

Zoey leaned forward. "Do you like it as much as

you thought you would in real life?" she had to ask.

Libby held the dress up and turned it back and forth, so it twirled, and shook her head.

"No?" *Really?* Zoey thought to herself. "Oh . . . I'm sor—" she began. Maybe it was a good thing she didn't enter it after all.

"I like it *better*!" Libby said, hugging it to her. "It's so me! It's like the dress I never knew I always wanted."

"In that case, I'm calling it the 'Libby dress' on my blog!" Zoey said, relieved.

"Well, it's an official Sew Zoey, too," Libby said, pulling up the collar to see the label. "See?"

"Okay, now I'm really jealous," Kate said.

Zoey and Libby turned to her, dumbfounded.

"But . . . I thought you didn't like dresses, Kate." Zoey gulped.

Kate grinned. "Just kidding! You're too easy!" She laughed and shook her head.

Zoey laughed nervously, but she also remembered something. "Hey! I *do* have something for you. And you." She pointed to Kate and Libby.

"Priti, too?" Kate asked.

"Yep. Can you guys come over after school?" she asked.

Libby nodded, but Kate did not. Instead, she pointed to the cleats tied to her overstuffed backpack.

"After school *and* after your soccer game?" Zoey corrected herself at once. No way, she knew, could she and her friends miss another one. "We'll go watch you play first."

Kate smiled, and it spread to all of them. Zoey's was bigger than it had been in days.

Her friend patches had worked, she thought. (Though she *still* had to do her jeans.)

Of all the soccer games to go to, that day's was not the best. Mapleton lost, 3 to 1, but Kate scored a goal, at least.

Back at Zoey's house, she led her friends to her bedroom, where she'd stowed the box of Cecily Chen's clothes.

"Are you ready?" she asked as she pulled back the top flaps.

"What is it?" Priti asked.

"Oh . . ." Zoey whisked out a baby-blue boatneck top and waved it before them, like a bull fighter's cape. "Just a few original samples from Cecily Chen's new not-even-in-stores-yet tween line!"

They all sat there like mannequins, speechless. Priti finally found her voice.

"Where'd you get them?!" she demanded, leaping to her feet.

"She sent them to me!" Zoey replied.

Priti started to squeal as she peered in the box.

"Oh my gosh! That's so cool!" Libby cried, jumping up.

"What else is in there?!" Kate asked.

"Show us! Show us!" Priti and Libby both begged.

One by one, Zoey took out every precious garment and passed them out to her friends. To Priti, she gave the lavender miniskirt layered with tulle. To Kate, she gave the sunny yellow jeans and slouchy gray tunic. To Libby, she gave the pink boatneck top with the flutter-sleeves.

"Oh my gosh! It's so cute!" Libby said as she took it. "Almost as cute as the dress *you* made!"

"I still have no idea who Cecily Chen is," Kate

declared. "All I know is I love this shirt!"

"We should thank her!" said Priti.

"Great idea!" Zoey agreed. "Let's do it. Let's send her an e-mail right now."

She scooped up her laptop and pulled up her e-mail—and that's when she noticed the bold, new unread mail in her in-box from the sender Avalon.

"What's wrong?" Kate asked.

"There's an e-mail here . . . from Avalon Fabrics . . . about the contest," Zoey said.

"Already? Yippee!" said Libby.

"Well, open it, Zo!" Priti said.

Zoey winced. "I'm afraid to."

"Why?" Libby asked.

Zoey lowered the top of her laptop with both hands. "What if it says something bad?"

"Oh, Zo! Open it!" Priti told her. "You have to. If you don't, I will."

"I'm sure it will be good," said Kate.

"Me too," Libby chimed in.

Zoey wasn't so sure herself, but whatever news she got, maybe it was better to get it now, she thought . . . so she could share it with her friends.

Slowly, she opened the computer again. The other girls crossed their fingers as she did. Zoey scooted the cursor over the Avalon e-mail, then she took a deep breath and clicked.

"Well?" said Priti.

"What does it say?" asked Libby.

"*Zo!* Tell us!" demanded Kate.

Zoey nodded, but read the message through again first, just to make sure she understood it.

She smiled and looked around at her friends. "I . . . ," she began.

"Oh my gosh! You won! You won! You won!" Priti cried.

"Yay!" Libby and Kate grabbed each other's hands and started to dance around the bed.

"Wait!" Zoey raised her hand to try to get their attention. "Hang on," she said calmly.

"What?" Gradually, they all settled down and turned to her.

"You did win, right?" said Kate.

Zoey shook her head, and all three jaws fell open wide.

"You didn't?" Priti stuck out her lip.

"Are you serious? Those judges don't know any-thing!" Kate said. She glanced at Libby. "No offense."

"No, you're right!" Libby said, frowning. "I'm so sorry, Zoey. I'm calling my aunt tonight and telling her what a huge mistake she made. That was such a great dress. I can't believe it didn't win."

"Aw, I'm so sorry," Priti said, draping her arm around Zoey's neck.

Zoey leaned against her, but she was still smil-ing. "Hang on, guys. I didn't win—but I didn't lose either. Yet. Listen." She quickly cleared her throat—"Ah-hem"—and read:

Dear Zoey Webber,

Thank you for participating in Avalon Fabrics' Break-Out Designer contest. As you can imagine, our esteemed judges have been hard at work reviewing the more than 250 entries received, and we are most pleased, therefore, to inform you that your design has been chosen to advance to the regional round.

"The regional round? What's that?" said Kate.

"It's like a semifinal, I guess," Zoey said. "It says

there'll be a ceremony—Oh, look! Awesome! It's at A Stitch in Time! And then they'll announce a regional winner, to move on to the final round."

"So, that's good, right?!" said Priti.

"That's great!" Libby said.

"When's the ceremony?" Kate asked.

Zoey checked. "Next week!"

"That's torture!" said Priti.

"Not really," Zoey said. "Not having you guys as friends was torture. Waiting for this will be a piece of cake."

CHAPTER 13

Confetti Confessions

So tonight's the big night!!!! I've been on pins and needles all day! This is what I've decided to wear after trying on a million things. I even added glitter to my ballet flats. I've really tried not to get my hopes up too high, but that's always hard for me. If you haven't noticed, my default attitude is hopeful! Am I jinxing it, do you think, picturing my dress on the racks at H. Cashin's next spring? Or is that just the kind of positive thinking every crazy dream needs? Don't worry. You will, of course, be the first to know how tonight turns out. I'd say wish me luck (like I always seem to do), but I'm feeling pretty lucky already, so for once I'm not going to. Why do I feel so lucky? I'm so glad you asked! Because I know that whatever happens, my best friends in the world will be by my side. And you couldn't get much luckier than that if you tried. I feel like I already won!

"And now the moment we've all been waiting for!"

Jan stood at the center of her store, where a podium had been set up. She was wearing her hair particularly high, and her outfit was particularly loud: a shiny, bright-fuchsia silk blouse over a sleek leopard skirt. Jan made everything she wore, and it was all very Jan.

The place was full. There were five finalists, plus their family and friends. There were also dozens of regular A Stitch in Time customers.

Zoey was by far the youngest of the five contestants. The others looked in their twenties, at least. Two were men and two were women, and they all looked equally anxious to see who would be the regional winner. All five contest entries were prominently displayed just inside the front door. Zoey could easily see any one being sold in H. Cashin's.

She'd found a place to stand by the button racks, not far from the podium, with her friends. It was such a relief to be friends again, and they all showed up to support Zoey. Libby was wearing the "Libby dress" (she would have worn it every day if she could), and Priti and Kate were in Cecily Chen. Zoey's dad stood behind her in his bright new tie and his goofy but sweet fatherly smile. Marcus had on his usual ensemble—jeans and a T-shirt—and the look of a proud older brother.

"And our regional winner is . . ."

The girls squeezed one another's hands and tightly closed their eyes.

"Roland Lopez!"

Zoey felt the hands in hers get looser as she somberly raised her head.

"Congratulations, Roland!" Jan said. A man with a big smile on his face glided to the front of the room and shook her hand.

Kate put her arm across Zoey's shoulders, and Priti put her arm around Zoey's waist. Libby looked at her and sighed, then took a deep breath and sighed again.

"Oh well," said Zoey wearily. Of course, she knew it was a long shot, but she still wanted to win. She watched Roland grin as the crowd applauded him and wished she were up there in his place.

"I'm so excited for Roland, aren't you?" Jan went on, patting his arm. "But you other four, you're not leaving empty-handed. Don't you worry. Avalon Fabrics has some prizes for you!" She picked four envelopes up off the podium and waved them high above her head. "Michelle Winkler, Julie Tse, Alex Nielson, and Zoey Webber, come on up!"

"What do you think it is?" asked Priti.

Zoey shook her head. "I have no idea. . . ."

She was the first to reach Jan, who opened her arms wide and wrapped Zoey in a hug.

"Oh, Zoey! I can't tell you how proud I am of

you! I could have seen you going all the way!" She pressed an envelope into Zoey's hand and gave her another squeeze. "Have fun with this, missy."

Zoey made her way back to her friends, with the envelope clutched tightly between her fingers.

"What is it? What'd you get?" they asked her.

"I don't know," Zoey said.

"Well, open it!" Priti ordered her.

"Maybe it's an H. Cashin's gift card?" Libby guessed.

Zoey lifted the tab of the envelope and pulled out a stiff gray-and-gold certificate.

"It's a gift certificate for Avalon Fabrics," Zoey said as she read it. "Five hundred dollars . . . Oh my gosh! That's a *lot*!" She raised the card to her lips and kissed it. *Mwah!* Then she hugged it and beamed at her friends. "Put in your orders now, guys!" she declared. "I'm going on a fabric shopping spree!"

That night, Zoey was feeling pretty good, even though she didn't win. The icing on the cake was when she checked her blog. A reader named LibbysAuntNYC had posted a comment:

Hi, Zoey! I was one of the judges for Avalon's contest and wanted you to know that we loved your dress! It was so creative, but just too hard to mass produce, and maybe not quite right for our consumer. All that said, you should be very proud of your work. Keep sewing, Zoey.

Zoey was on cloud nine. Libby's aunt had gone to the trouble to explain why she didn't win the contest. It must have been a tough decision. Wow!

She was feeling pretty awesome—almost as awesome as if she had won—and spent the rest of the night thinking about what she would make with five hundred dollars' worth of fabric. Every so often, she clicked the button to refresh her blog page, so she could read the latest comments from Sew Zoey followers.

The congratulations kept coming. Zoey fell asleep to the glow of the laptop screen, dreaming of endless rows of fabric and twirling dress forms. Now *that* was awesome.

Don't miss a stitch . . .
of the story!

Turn the page for a
sneak peek at the next
Sew Zoey book:

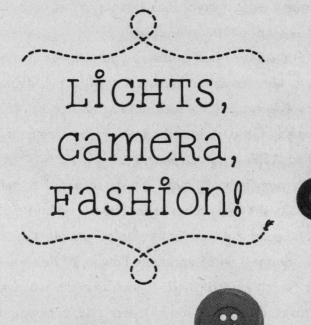

LIGHTS,
CAMERA,
FASHION!

To Thine Own Self Be . . . Blue?

When I thought seventh grade would be so much better than sixth grade, I forgot that CERTAIN PEOPLE— mostly one certain person—would still think their job is to make life at Mapleton Prep difficult. Everyone always says you just have to ignore those people, but it's not easy, because they're in school every day. When I feel blue about it, Dad says I should follow Shakespeare's advice and "Above all, to thine own self be true", which is a fancy way of telling me to be myself and stop caring so much what everyone else thinks. It's easy for him to say—he's not in middle school.

Speaking of being true to yourself, Aunt Lulu took me to see a Frida Kahlo exhibit at the art museum over the weekend. Her life was so sad, but her art, WOW! It jumped off the walls and hit you in the face as if it was saying, "This is me. Deal with it!"

Anyway, what I loved the most was that her self-portraits showed off her style: She mixed and matched bright colors, paired embroidered square tunics with lace-trimmed skirts, and wore flowers or ribbons in her hair (which kind of made it look like she was wearing a crown, at least, to me.) I loved it all, and would give just about anything to go shopping in her closet. And I totally want to wear flowers in my hair from now on.

I also want to go to Mexico someday to visit Frida Kahlo's house, La Casa Azul. There are so many places I want to go! But the only place I can go right now is to bed. Dad just shouted "lights out" since it's a school night. Feeling less blue already! Thanks for listening.

"I think you're going to love this one," Ms. Brown said, winking at Zoey as she handed her a copy of the next class read. Zoey turned the book over. When she saw the title, The Misfits, her heart sank. Language Arts was her favorite class and her teacher, Ms. Brown, one of the few who seemed to really understand her. Did Ms. Brown think she was a misfit?

Zoey turned to the description on the back of the book and scanned the synopsis, and she thought, "Okay, maybe it's worth a try."

Just then the loudspeaker hissed to life. "Good morning, Mapleton Prep students," Ms. Austen's melodious voice crackled. "I have a special annoucement. The upcoming fall dance is going to be a Sadie Hawkins Dance."

From the murmurs of "What's that?" and "Sadie who?" Zoey could tell she wasn't the only one who didn't know what that meant.

"A Sadie Hawkins Dance is also called a Vice Versa dance, because instead of the boys asking the girls to the dance it's vice versa. Tickets go on sale tomorrow," Ms. Austen continued.

The class erupted as soon as the announcement ended.

"Why do we have to wait for the girls to ask us?" Joe Latrone complained. "That's not fair!"

"Do we have to ask a boy?" Shannon asked. "Can we just wait for them to ask us?"

"You don't have to ask a boy," Ms. Brown told her. "You can go with a group of friends. And Joe, why is it any more fair for a girl to wait for you to ask her?"

"I don't know," Joe shrugged. "That's how it usually happens."

"Well, this time it'll happen differently," Ms. Brown said. "If we always stuck to the status quo, we'd still have slavery and women wouldn't have the vote. Sometimes change is good."

Ms. Brown started class, but as soon they broke into their small group discussions, talk turned to the dance and what to wear. Ivy was in the group next to Zoey's. Zoey heard her boasting that she had the perfect dress. Zoey wondered what that looked like.

Suddenly Ivy turned around and said, "I bet you're going to turn up in one of those stupid craft projects from your blog. That'll attract a lot of dates!"

Zoey lifted her chin and tried to ignore Ivy and the giggles she heard from the other kids in Ivy's group, which hurt her just as much. She tried to remind herself of all the great comments she got about her designs from her blog readers.

"I'll go with Zoey," said a voice. Zoey turned to see who it was. . . .